Manfred Karge
THE CONQUEST OF THE
SOUTH POLE

translated by Anthony Vivis

MAN TO MAN

ROYAL COURT WRITERS SERIES

First published as a paperback original in 1988 by Methuen Drama, Michelin House,
81 Fulham Road, London SW3 6RB and distributed in the United States of America by
HEB Inc., 70 Court Street, Portsmouth, New Hampshire 03801, USA

British Library Cataloguing in Publication Data
Karge, Manfred
    Man to man; and, conquest of the South Pole
    I. Title   II.Karge, Manfred. Conquest of
    the South Pole   III. Jacke wie Hose.
    IV. Eroberung des Sudpols.
    English
    832'.914

    ISBN 0-413-61200-7

Printed in Great Britain by Expression Printers Ltd, London N7 9DP

CAUTION
All rights whatsoever in these plays are strictly reserved and application for performance etc.
should be made before rehearsals start to Rosica Colin Limited of 1 Clareville Grove Mews,
London SW7 5AH. No performances may be given unless a licence has been obtained.

COMING NEXT

IN THE MAIN HOUSE   730 1745

Sunday 20 November at 7.30pm

DOWNSHIRE PLAYERS OF LONDON

associate orchestra at the Royal Court Theatre

Conductor: Peter Ash   Violin: Tina Gruenberg
Janis Kelly: (Soprano)   Viola: Paul Silverthorne
Geoffrey Dolton: (Baritone)

The Downshire Players of London return to the Royal Court after their highly
successful concert in August with a programme of music by Haydn and Mozart.

IN THE THEATRE UPSTAIRS   730 2554

22 November - 10 December

BRISTOL OLD VIC and
THE ROYAL COURT THEATRE present

INVENTING A NEW COLOUR

by Paul Godfrey
Directed by Phyllida Lloyd

An Exeter family take in an evacuee from London during heavy raids on their city
in 1942. His presence confirms their sense of isolation as the world threatens to
change forever. A disturbing, poetic play about loss: of innocence, of ambition
and of a future.

10 - 28 January

The Royal Court Young People's Theatre presents

A ROCK IN WATER

by Winsome Pinnock
Directed by Elyse Dodgson

From 16 February

The Women's Playhouse Trust in association with
the Royal Court Theatre present

A HERO'S WELCOME

by Winsome Pinnock.
Directed by Jules Wright

THE NEW PATRONAGE SCHEME
AT THE ROYAL COURT

For many years now Members of the Royal Court Theatre Society have received special notice of new productions, but why not consider contributing £35 (or £50 joint membership) and become a **Friend of the Royal Court** — or approach your company or business to become an **Associate** or a **Patron**, thereby involving yourself directly in maintaining the high standard and unique quality of Royal Court productions — while enjoying complimentary tickets to the shows themselves?

1 MEMBERSHIP SCHEME
For £10 you will receive details of all forthcoming events via the Royal Court *Member's Letter*, and be entitled to purchase any available seat for £3 during previews (maximum of two per Member).

2 FRIENDS
OF THE ROYAL COURT
For £35 (or £50 joint membership) you will be entitled to one (or two) complimentary preview ticket(s) for performances on the Main Stage and one (or two) preview tickets for productions in the Theatre Upstairs. You will automatically be on our mailing list and be invited to all lectures and special events.

3 ASSOCIATES
OF THE ROYAL COURT
For £350 you will be entitled to four top price tickets (previews or press nights) to all Main House productions and two tickets to all plays in the Theatre Upstairs.

4 PATRONS
For £1,000 you can make a 'personal appearance' on a plaque in the Royal Court lobby, and appear in our programme. In addition, you will be entitled to six free tickets for four shows in the Main House or the Theatre Upstairs.

When you have chosen from the four categories, please make your cheque/P.O. payable to the *Royal Court Theatre Society* and send to: *Max Stafford-Clark, Artistic Director, Royal Court Theatre, Sloane Square, London SW1*. Alternatively, if you wish to covenant for four years or more by filling in the form which you will find in the theatre foyer, we — as a registered charity — can claim back the tax you have already paid, thereby increasing the value of your donation.

PATRONS
Caryl Churchill, Mrs. Henny Gestetner, Tracey Ullman

ASSOCIATES
Richard Barran, David Capelli, Michael Codron, Elizabeth Garvie, Patricia Marmont, Barbara Minto, David Mirvish, Greville Poke, Sir Dermot de Trafford, Richard Wilson.

FRIENDS
Robin Anderson, Jan Annakin, John Arthur, Mrs. M. Bagust, Linda Bassett, Bob Boas, Katie Bradford, Jim Broadbent, Alan Brodie, A. J. H. Buckley, Guy Chapman, Angela Coles, Miss C. Collingwood, Jeremy Conway, Lou Coulson, Peter Cregeen, Charles Dance, Alan David, Mrs. Der Pao Graham, Anne Devlin, Ann Diamond, R. H. & B. H. Dowler, Adrian Charles Dunbar, Susan Dunnett, George A. Elliott III, Jan Evans, Trevor Eve, Kenneth Ewing, Kate Feast, Gilly Fraser, David Gant, Kerry Gardner, Anne Garwood, Jonathan Gems, Lord Goodman, Audrey and Gordon Taylor, Rod Hall, Sharon Hamper, Jan Harvey, Jocelyn Herbert, Dusty Hughes, Kenny Ireland, Alison E. Jackson, Dominic Jephcott, Paul Jesson, Elizabeth Karr Tashman, Sharon Kean, Dr. R. J. Lande, Iain Lanyon, Sheila Lemon, Suzie Mackenzie, Barbara Mackie, Marina Martin, Paul Matthews, Philip L. McDonald, John Nicolls, Nick Marston, Richard O'Brien, Donal O'Leary, Stephen Oliver, Gary Olsen, Ronald Pickup, Pauline Pinder, Harold Pinter, Margaret Ramsay, Jane Rayne, Alan Rickman, Dr. P. A. Rixon, David Robb, A. J. Sayers, Mrs. L. M. Sieff, Paul Sinclair Brooks, Louise Stein, Lindsay Stevens, Richard Stokes, Richard Stone, Rob Sutherland, Nigel Terry, Mary Trevelyan, Mrs. Anne Underwood, Maureen Vincent, Julian Wadham, Harriet Walter, Julie Walters, Julia M. Walters, Sarah Wheatland.

FOR THE ROYAL COURT

DIRECTION

Artistic Director..MAX STAFFORD-CLARK
Deputy Director..SIMON CURTIS
Director of the Theatre Upstairs...LINDSAY POSNER
Assistant Director...PHILIP HOWARD
Casting Director..LISA MAKIN
Literary Manager..KATE HARWOOD
Senior Script Associate...MICHAEL HASTINGS*
Resident Playwright...HARWANT S. BAINS*
Artistic Assistant...MELANIE KENYON

PRODUCTION

Production Manager..BO BARTON
Technical Manager, Theatre Upstairs.......................................CHRIS BAGUST
Chief Electrician...COLIN ROXBOROUGH
Deputy Chief Electrician...MARK BRADLEY
Electrician...DENIS O'HARE*
Sound Designer...BRYAN BOWEN
Acting Master Carpenter...JOHN BURGESS
Acting Deputy Carpenter..MATTHEW SMITH
Wardrobe Supervisor..JENNIFER COOK
Deputy Wardrobe Supervisor..CATHIE SKILBECK

ADMINISTRATION

General Manager...GRAHAM COWLEY
Assistant to General Manager...LUCY WOOLLATT
Finance Administrator..STEPHEN MORRIS
Finance Assistant...GILL RUSSELL
Press Manager..SALLY LYCETT
Marketing & Publicity Manager...GUY CHAPMAN
Development Director..TOM PETZAL
Development Assistant...JACQUELINE VIEIRA
Acting House Manager...ALISON SMITH
Bookshop Manager...DIANE PETHERICK*
Box Office Manager...STEVEN CURRIE
Box Office Assistants...........................GERALD BROOKING, ROSALEEN DEW
Box Office Trainee..RITA SHARMA*
Stage Door/Telephonists.......................DIANE PETHERICK*, CERI SHIELDS*
Evening Stage Door...TYRONE LUCAS*
Maintenance...JOHN LORRIGIO*
Cleaners...EILEEN CHAPMAN*, IVY JONES*
Firemen.......................................MARK BRYERS*, PAUL KLEINMANN*

YOUNG PEOPLE'S THEATRE

Director...ELYSE DODGSON
Temporary Administrator...DOMINIC TICKELL

*Part-time staff

This Theatre is associated with the Thames Television Playwright Scheme, and the Regional Theatre Young Directors Scheme

FOR THE TRAVERSE:

Chairman	SHEENA McDONALD
General Manager	ANNE BONNAR
Artistic Director	IAN BRO.VN
Assistant to the Artistic Director	JANE ELLIS
Production Manager	ROB FLOWER
Press and Publicity	ALAN POLLOCK
Assistant General Manager	KATIE STUART
Accountant	HEATHER THOMSON
SAC Assistant Director	BEN TWIST
Box Office Manager	KAREN WINNING

The Traverse would like to thank:

U.Y.C. Ltd — The First Name in Catering and Baking in Scotland; Lynben Ltd — Gailforce Garments; Nevisport Ltd; Blues Ski Shop; Alloa Brewery Co. Ltd for the Lowenbrau; Valvona and Crolla — Italian Wine Specialists; Nevica Sports Wear; Alice Louise Tarbuck; John Paton — Potato Merchant; John Bryden — Florist; Goodwin's Antiques; The Royal Blind Asylum; St Ivel's Creamery; Broxburn; H. Samuel; Murray Seaton's Drum Shop; Fairfield Dairy; Gateway Superstore; Macgregor's Glass and China; Carson Clark Gallery — Map Specialist; Turnbull and Wilson Ltd — Household Textiles; Campbell Medical Supplies; Blossom's, Viewforth; Charles Burns International Newsagents; Edinburgh Univesity Geography Dept.; Waterstone and Co. Ltd; Bandparts Music Stores Ltd; W. & A. Gilbey Ltd; R.J. Reynolds Tobacco; Wm. Low and Co. Ltd; Field and Stream; Ian Russell — Paints; Dofo's Pet Centres; Mackenzie's Sports; Nature's Gate; China Cave; Graham Tiso's; The Scout Shop; Asda Stores; Herby's Delicatessen; Lyons Coffee; Kent Cigarettes supplied by Astran and Seita; the North British Hotel; Party Poppers donated by Sohni (Esco) Ltd — Fireworks; British Antarctic Survey Unit; Rowntree Mackintosh; E.B. Forrest and Co. Antiques; Wardrobe care by Persil and Comfort.

The Traverse Production of CONQUEST OF THE SOUTH POLE received financial assistance from the Goethe Institut, Glasgow.

THE CONQUEST OF THE SOUTH POLE

by Manfred Karge

Translated by Tinch Minter and Anthony Vivis

SLUPIANEK .... Alan Cumming
BUESCHER .... Paul Higgins
SEIFFERT *nicknamed*
The Moose of Herne .... Alastair Galbraith
BRAUKMANN .... Sam Graham
LA BRAUKMANN .... Carol Ann Crawford
FRANKIEBOY .... Ewen Bremner
RUDI .... Simon Donald
ROSI .... Hilary Maclean

Directed by .... Stephen Unwin
Designed by .... Lucy Weller
Assistant Directors .... Paul Miller and
Tilda Swinton
Lighting and Sound by .... George Tarbuck
Music by .... Alastair Galbraith
and Paul Higgins
Company Voice Work .... Carol Ann Crawford
Company Stage Manager .... Sarah Jane Kerr
Deputy Stage Manager .... Jacqui Jeffrey
Assistant Stage Manager .... Suzy Stamp
Publicity Photographs .... Sean Hudson
Production Photographs .... John Haynes
Poster and Leaflet Design .... Simon Williams

Set and costumes made in the Traverse Workshop and Wardrobe

THERE WILL BE NO INTERVAL

The British Premiere of THE CONQUEST OF THE SOUTH POLE was at
the Traverse Theatre, Edinburgh, on 16 July 1988.

Wardrobe care by PERSIL and BIO-TEX. Adhesive by COPYDEX and EVODE LTD. Ioniser for the lighting control room by THE LONDON IONISER CENTRE (836 0211). Cordless drill by MAKITA ELECTRIC (UK) LTD. Watches by THE TIMEX CORPORATION. Batteries by EVER READY, refrigerators by ELECTROLUX and PHILLIPS MAJOR APPLIANCIES LTD. Microwaves by TOSHIBA UK LTD. Kettles for rehearsals by MORPHY RICHARDS. Television for backstage by GRANADA. Video for casting purposes by HITACHI. Sound desk by CADAC. Cold bottled beers at the bar supplied by YOUNG & CO. BREWERY, WANDSWORTH. Coffee machines by CONA.

Funded by

LONDON BOROUGHS GRANTS SCHEME

FINANCIALLY ASSISTED BY THE
ROYAL BOROUGH OF
KENSINGTON AND CHELSEA

WITH ASSISTANCE FROM THE
GOETHE-INSTITUT LONDON

Arts Council Funded

Biographies

EWEN BREMNER   Theatre includes: *No More Sitting on the Old School Bench* (Brunton Theatre); *Has Anybody Seen Joe?* (Theatre Workshop, Edinburgh); *The Conquest of the South Pole* (Traverse Theatre); *The Funeral* (Tron Theatre Co.). Films: *Heavenly Pursuits* and *The Riveter*.

CAROL ANN CRAWFORD   Theatre includes: *Daisy Pulls It Off* (Globe Theatre); for the Contact Theatre, Manchester: *Oh What A Lovely War!*, *Arturo Ui*, *Scrap*, *Crystal Clear*, *After Mafeking*; for the Traverse Theatre: *Elizabeth Gordon Quinn*, *Losing Venice* (also in Australia, Sweden, Hong Kong, and at the Almeida Theatre), *Elias Sawney*, *The Conquest of the South Pole*; *Killing Time* (The Mill at Sonning); for the Theatre Royal, York: *Our Day Out*, *The Good Woman of Setzuan*. Recent television: *House on the Hill*, *Odyssey*, *The Mother Tongue*. Films: *Another Time Another Place*, *Every Picture Tells a Story*.

ALAN CUMMING   Recent theatre includes: for the Tron Theatre: *Macbeth*, *Macbeth Possessed*, *Sleeping Beauty*, *Babes in the Wood*; for the Royal Lyceum, Edinburgh: *Tartuffe*, *A Streetcar Named Desire*, *Mr. Government*; for the Dundee Rep: *The Slab Boys*, *Cuttin' A Rug*; *The Conquest of the South Pole* (Traverse Theatre). Television: *Travelling Man*, *Taggart*, *Shadow of the Stone*, *Take the High Road*, *Let's See*. Film: *Passing Glory*. Cabaret: *Victor and Barry*.

SIMON DONALD   Recent theatre includes: for the Traverse Theatre: *Losing Venice*, *Elizabeth Gordon Quinn*, *Prickly Heat* (which he also wrote), *The Conquest of the South Pole*; *The Park* (Crucible Theatre). Author of: *In Descent* (Traverse Theatre); *A Tenant for Edgar Mortez* (Abattoir Theatre Co.). Co-founder Abattoir Theatre Company.

ALASTAIR GALBRAITH   Theatre: *David Copperfield* (Edinburgh Festival); *In Camera* (Edinburgh Festival Fringe); *Bench at the Edge* (Edinburgh Festival Fringe); *The Slab Boys* (Unit Theatre Co.); *Aladdin* (Citizens' Theatre); for TAG Theatre Co.: *Visible Differences*, *Joe*, *Great Expectations*; *The Conquest of the South Pole* (Traverse). Television: *City Lights*, *Arena*.

SAM GRAHAM   Recent Theatre: *Loot* (Druid Theatre Co.); for the Traverse Theatre: *The Prowler*, *Dead Dad Dog*, *The Way We Were*, *The Conquest of the South Pole*. Television: *Bergerac*, *All at No. 20*. Film: *Heavenly Pursuits*.

PAUL HIGGINS   Theatre: *The Lemmings are Coming* (Riverside Studios); *A Wholly Healthy Glasgow* (Royal Exchange, Edinburgh Festival, Royal Court); *The Conquest of the South Pole* (Traverse). Television: *Taggart*, *A Wholly Healthy Glasgow*, *A Very Peculiar Practice*, *Tumbledown*.

HILARY MACLEAN   Recent theatre: *Trivial Pursuits* (Lyceum Theatre, Edinburgh); for Brunton Theatre: *Cabaret*, *Prime of Miss Jean Brodie*, *Jungle Book*; *The Conquest of the South Pole* (Traverse). Television: *Taggart*, *City Lights*, *Biting the Hand*, *Channel 4's Hogmanay Show*.

GEORGE TARBUCK   Has worked extensively in both Britain and Europe as Stage Manager, Lighting Director, special effects and explosives consultant. He is resident Lighting Designer at the Traverse and has lit the majority of the Traverse shows during the last five years.

STEPHEN UNWIN   Productions at the Traverse include: *Barry*, *Sandra/Manon* (transferred Donmar Warehouse), *White Rose*, (transferred Almeida), *Elizabeth Gordon Quinn*, *Elias Sawney*, *The Orphans' Comedy*, *Kathie and the Hippotamus* (transferred Almeida), *Man to Man* (transferred Royal Court), *Dead Dad Dog* (transferred Royal Court), *The Conquest of the South Pole*; for the National Theatre Studio: *The Lottery of Love*, *Torquato Tasso*, *A Yorkshire Tragedy*; *The Decision* (Almeida Music Festival); *Look*.

LUCY WELLER   Recent designs include: *Great Expectations* (TAG Theatre Company); *Berlin Days*, *Hollywood Nights* (Paines Plough); *The Pilot's Tale* and *The Martyrdom of Saint Magnus* (Opera Factory); *The Decision* (Almeida); *Food Stuff* and *Please Please Please* (Theatre de Complicite). For the Traverse: *The Silver Sprig* and *Elias Sawney*. For the Royal Court: *Low Level Panic* and the 1988 Young Writers' Festival.

About The Traverse

Tilda Swinton in Manfred Karge's MAN TO MAN.
Photo by Sean Hudson

HAPPY END Photo by Alan Daicles

Edinburgh's tiny 100 seat theatre — the first studio theatre in the world — has this year been celebrating an improbable anniversary. The Traverse opened, 25 years ago, in a former brothel off the Royal Mile, where a handful of subscribers gathered on a bitterly cold night in January 1963 to watch the opening production— Sartre's *Huis Clos*. On the second night, the accidental on-stage stabbing of the leading actress propelled the fledgling theatre club into the headlines, where, by one means or another, it has since remained.

Born out of the euphoria of the early Edinburgh Fringe — and the Quixotic vision of a small group of committed individuals — the Theatre has survived, against all the odds, to become the only Theatre outside London entirely dedicated to the production of new British and international work. In the last quarter century it has launched the careers of some of our best-known writers, actors, directors and designers.

In the words of the critic, Michael Billington, the Traverse has "profoundly affected both the architecture and the ethos of modern theatre. Exactly like the Royal Court, the Traverse has an influence on our culture totally out of proportion to its size or its subsidy. The health of our television, film and theatre stems from the obstinate faith in writers shown by companies like the Traverse . . . "

The roll-call of writers whose first, or early works, were seen at the Traverse reads like a Who's Who of British theatre: Howard Barker, Peter Barnes, Steven Berkoff, Howard Brenton, John Byrne, David Edgar, Marcella Evaristi, Trevor Griffiths, David Hare, Robert Holman, Liz Lochhead, Claire Luckham, Tom McGrath, Mustapha Matura, Mike Stott, C.P. Taylor, Michael Wilcox and Heathcote Williams.

Manfred Karge's *The Conquest of the South Pole* is only the most recent in a long line of important international works premiered at the Traverse. The Theatre has given British premieres to plays by Bertolt Brecht, Saul Bellow, Marguerite Duras, Max Frisch, Günter Grass, Franz Xavier Kroetz, Yukio Mishima, Sam Shepard, Barney Simon, Michael Tremblay and Mario Vargas Llosa.

The Soviet playwright Alexander Gelman's *A Man With Connections* (premiered at the Traverse in August 1988) will be seen at the Royal Court in the New Year.

Over the years Traverse productions have transferred to theatres all over the world. The Royal Court itself set the trend in 1964 by taking Michael Geliot's spectacularly successful production of Brecht's *Happy End* — starring opera singer Bettina Jonic and with sets designed by the young Ralph Koltai and Nadine Bayliss.

Since then the Royal Court has welcomed a steady stream of Traverse productions — and one former Artistic Director in the shape of Max Stafford-Clark.

In 1978, with the transfer of *The Slab Boys*, Royal Court audiences were the first outside Scotland to witness the extraordinary talents of the Glasgow writer/artist John Byrne — whose *Tutti Frutti* has been the undisputed highlight of recent television drama. In January, Tilda Swinton's stunning solo performance of Manfred Karge's *Man to Man* was hailed by The Listener as 'one of the theatrical feats of a turbulent decade'.

The driving force behind the Traverse has always been that of change. The Theatre has been through many different incarnations in the 25 years since 1963 and, as the Traverse nears the end of its Silver Jubilee year, it is preparing to reinvent itself once again, with the departure of Jenny Killick and the appointment of Ian Brown as Artistic Director.

In 3 years time the Theatre will take its boldest step since the move from former brothel to former sailmaker's loft in 1969 — by taking up residence in a brand-new space on the site of Edinburgh's notorious Hole-in-the-Ground. The New Traverse will be the first new theatre built in Edinburgh this century and the first purpose-built new writing theatre ever in Britain.

Introduction to the plays

Karge writes about the Germany he knows — a single country divided. He was born in the DDR, and is still a citizen of that country. It was there he had his theatrical training and, through his experience of Brecht, learnt how to give dramatic potency to his critical view of society. It was only after he has been living in the West for six years that he wrote his first play: *Jacke Wie Hose*. The German title translated literally — 'Six of one and half a dozen of the other' — suggests that both systems fail the individual.

Britain is on the one hand not as prosperous West Germany, nor on the other ever likely to become a socialist state. Yet the way Karge fuses his experiences of the two Germanys speaks directly to British audiences. Whatever the politics, he focuses on the individual, often in conflict with the state. In a male-dominated world which actively represses the individual, Ella/Max in *Man to Man* must fight if she is to survive. Conditions force her to adopt her dead husband's persona. Similarly, the four no-hopers in *The Conquest of the South Pole* must replace their hopelessness with something worth living for, however imaginary.

In these two plays, nothing drains an individual's self-esteem more than unemployment. The central characters in *The Conquest of the South Pole* find that their own personae are rejected by society. They search for dignity by getting into the skins of Antarctic explorers. In both plays, the main characters are eccentric because they are unable to act from the fullness of their personalities. With our love of eccentricity, especially when it cocks a snook at authority, audiences here warm to Karge's characters.

In this country unemployment is familiar territory, but one which embarrasses us to the point of not wishing to talk about it and certainly not using it as a basis for comedy. By giving this dangerous subject a comic treatment, Karge ensures it is not beneath our contempt. The irony of Ella/Max's situation, the satire directed against the status quo in both plays, the anarchic inventiveness and sheer incongruity of some of the characters' responses — are all fundamental elements of British comic tradition.

One of Karge's techniques is akin to British understatement and takes a number of forms. At the end of Section 15 of *Man to Man*, Karge uses only one and a half lines to demolish the belief he has built up in the audience that Ella/Max is a victim of Nazism. With a deft dramatic shock effect, he reveals the reality: she's got away with playing an SA-man. In *The Conquest of the South Pole*, la Braukmann's taunt to Braukmann: 'South Pole traveller in the fridge' epitomises several of her frustrations while blowing the gaff on the men's fantasy world. Most important of all, perhaps, Karge provides only the most minimal of stage directions. In *Man to Man* numbered sections replace scenes. And in *The Conquest of the South Pole* time, place or stage furnishings are often indicated by a single word. This gives performer and director alike the greatest freedom of interpretation to 'translate' the plays into their own experience. And, in turn, allows the audience, liberated from the over-explicit naturalism of much modern theatre, to give their imagination free rein.

The Fool in *Lear* is a prototype of a stage character who does not need dignity or verbal adroitness to win our hearts. The stutterer, Frankieboy, in *The Conquest of the South Pole* can barely make an articulate sentence, but he makes the most powerful of emotional appeals. Natural compassion for the underdog leads us to identify with Karge's suffering characters. It is their failure — in society's eyes — which brings his people close to us. We sympathise with their failure, just as Buescher wants to play the role of Shackleton, because he failed to reach the Pole. We identify with their struggles, even though we know their achievements are based on the flimsiest foundations.

For us, part of the appeal of Karge's approach to theatre is that despite the spareness, even austerity, of his writing, he makes rich use of a host of theatrical effects. These include caricature, impersonation, and burlesque. And underlying all this is a didactic purpose, no weaker than it is in the work of Brecht or Bond. Like them, Karge can view a familiar situation analytically and demonstrate that what we can take for granted politically and socially is totally absurd.

Karge uses a *lingua franca* all his own. Much of the vocabulary in *The Conquest of the South Pole* would not appear in a standard German dicationary. And Ella/Max — a manual worker — is as likely to speak iambic pentameters as the no-hopers are to use alliteration. Often, the characters' attempts to hold on to their idividuality is expressed in wordplay or through references beyond their immediate experience: myth, fairy tale, historical event, or quotation.

At first the combination of literary allusion and street language may seem artificial. Yet this very disparity channels our attention to Karge's recurring theme, our inability to centre ourselves. And it is most often through the banality of modern life that he expresses the highest human aspirations.

Tinch Minter, Anthony Vivis.

Photograph of MANFRED KARGE taken at the Traverse Theatre, August 1988
by Chris Hill of Contact Photographers: (031) 228 2827

THE CONQUEST OF THE SOUTH POLE

The Conquest of the South Pole was first performed at the Traverse Theatre, Edinburgh, on 16 July 1988 and transferred to the Royal Court Theatre, London, on 17 November 1988, with the following cast:

SLUPIANEK	Alan Cumming
BÜSCHER	Paul Higgins
SEIFFERT nicknamed the Moose of Herne	Alastair Galbraith
BRAUKMANN	Sam Graham
LA BRAUKMANN	Carol Ann Crawford
FRANKIEBOY	Ewen Bremner
RUDI	Simon Donald
ROSI	Hilary Maclean

Directed by Stephen Unwin
Designed by Lucy Weller
Lighting by George Tarbuck

Scene One: The Moose in the Noose

The stage as a stage. A small red curtain.

SLUPIANEK. Can a camel ride a bike?

BÜSCHER.
BRAUKMANN. } No, no, no.

SLUPIANEK. Why not?

BÜSCHER.
BRAUKMANN. } Course not.

SLUPIANEK. Because, because, because –

BÜSCHER.
BRAUKMANN. } He's got no thumb to ring the bell.
SLUPIANEK.

SLUPIANEK. Where's Moose? Why can't I hear the greasy tones of his voice? Why can I only hear yours, Büscher, and yours, Braukmann, that's so thin? And I can also hear mine, my own, the voice of Slupianek. But I'm still missing Moose's mournful moo. What's keeping it? Right then, one more time lads.

BÜSCHER. } Can a camel ride a bike? –
BRAUKMANN. }   Why not? –
SLUPIANEK. } Because, because, because –

BÜSCHER. Wrong number.

BRAUKMANN. Here he isn't.

SLUPIANEK. Not a whiff of a Moose.

BÜSCHER. A scraplet of paper.

SLUPIANEK. What's on the scraplet of paper? Can the Moose have written us a note in his own unmistakable hoof? Playing pinball, lads, and all that. Büscher, what can you spy with your rusty little eye?

BRAUKMANN. It's so quiet. I can hear the waves washing the shores of the Volga.

BÜSCHER. Less lip, little 'un.

SLUPIANEK. You read it, Braukmann.

BRAUKMANN. I've mislaid my spectacles.

BÜSCHER. The news is mingy and moth-eaten, friends.

SLUPIANEK. Have I got to wait till Christmas?

BÜSCHER. I'll read. Final farewell to the jobcentre fullstop your ever loving Seiffert, called the Moose of Herne exclamation mark.

BRAUKMANN. Our pinball freak's freaked out.

SLUPIANEK. Claptrap. I fear the worst, friends, the worst is what I fear – A curtain. What's a curtain doing there? There's never been a curtain here before. The curtain wasn't here even yesterday.

BÜSCHER. What's behind the curtain?

SLUPIANEK. Paws off, Büscher. Behind this curtain, friends, behind this curtain that wasn't here even yesterday –

BRAUKMANN. What's behind the curtain that wasn't here even yesterday?

BÜSCHER. Speak, Slupianek. What's behind the curtain that we've never set eyes on before, but you keep staring at it as if it wasn't just a knicknack slung up by a nitwit? Speak, Slupianek, or I won't take my paws off.

SLUPIANEK. Friends, I'll tell you: behind this curtain that wasn't here even yesterday, and which, Büscher, you're going to take your paws off, is – let me describe it from bottom to top – behind this curtain, that we've never set eyes on here before, is a stool. But it's not standing to attention on its four sturdy legs, no, it's sprawling on the ground. Above it, floating in mid-air, a pair of shoes, brown, with gold laces. Then a pair of trousers, also brown and baggy, held up by a belt with a gold buckle. Next a shirt, green, with a fluorescent logo: Status Quo. Then a neck, scrawny. Round this neck which is scrawny, a noose, pulled tight. The Moose in a noose.

BRAUKMANN. The Moose in a noose.

BÜSCHER. The Moose.

SLUPIANEK. Yes, friends, the Moose. The Moose in a noose. Final farewell to the jobcentre, penny dropped, friends. And now we all know what's hiding behind this curtain, that wasn't here even yesterday, the time's come for me, Slupianek, to give the order: Braukmann, remove that rag.

SEIFFERT (*on a stool with a noose round his neck*). Hey, my three lovelies, Moose doesn't want to spoil your fun, but he says this: put the curtain back.

BRAUKMANN. Don't do anything silly, for Christ's sake.

SEIFFERT. Braukmann and Sons, put the curtain back.

SLUPIANEK. Come on, Moosy, we're off to play pinball. Come and join us. I bet you'll score 12,000 today easy as pie. My pee tells me. It's the kind of day when our Moose will clock up a breezy 12,000, easy as pie, we'll just stand there in awe, whilst our Moosy scores his breezy 12,000.

BRAUKMANN. Maybe fourteen.

BÜSCHER. Come on, Seiffert, help us paint the town red.

SEIFFERT. See my feeble grin, Büscher. Pinball, schnaps. It's old hat now, friends. Pinball, schnaps. Hanging around till the day of judgement. Pinball, schnaps. Eyeball to eyeball with a boring bunch like you. A finger on the flipper, a bottle in your gob. Clear off, Büscher, clear off, Braukmann, and you too, Slupianek, clear off. But to save me having to see your pathetic exit, please put the curtain back.

SLUPIANEK. Are you the only one hanging around?

BÜSCHER. Hanging around.

SLUPIANEK. Aren't we all jobless?

BÜSCHER. You've got to give something like this a lot of thought, Seiffert, a lot of thought.

BRAUKMANN. Right, Seiffert.

SLUPIANEK. I don't need helpful advice from you, because it isn't. Bugger off, me buckoes, and kindly put the curtain back.

BÜSCHER. Now he's really kicking up a stink, old Chunderguts there.

SLUPIANEK. Stop stirring, Büscher, you know the man's a rough diamond. Given time he'll get smooth. We're off then, Seiffert, you hear. I've dropped the Moose, we're off, but before we go we'll rig up your drapes for you. Curtain. End of the play. But no one claps, Seiffert, no one claps. Your audience is deaf, blind and unresponsive. And they've deposited their paws at the cloak-room. There's not a clap, Seiffert, or even a single boo. But, if I'm not mistaken, someone usually says a wordlet in front of the curtain, don't they, that's that, that's what it was about and so on. The moral of the story. Give us the moral of your story. Praps there'll be an encore. Explain yourself, you owe it to your public.

SEIFFERT. That's fine by me, Slupianek, I agree to say a few wordlets to you and the others right now. I can't see the point any more. Pinball, schnaps, the end. I've been reading a book.

BÜSCHER. Seiffert's been reading a book.

SEIFFERT. You can die laughing, Büscher, but I've been reading a book. About some hyper-rich types in France. You might think they have no problems, that's what you might think, but they have. It's called lennui, or something. Day and night they're up to their necks in this lennui. A kind of boredom, that's what it is. They don't get up till midday, but the lennui's already staring them in the face. They shovel in the caviare, and what are they thinking about, lennui. They have forty winks, get up, lennui.

BÜSCHER. Ah, the poor unemployed millionaires, they'll make me die laughing.

SLUPIANEK. Give the man a chance, Büscher, praps it'll get interesting. Go on, Seiffert, go on.

SEIFFERT. If a bunch like that, who've got all the answers, are driven to their needles and their hookahs by this lennui of theirs, what are poor buggers like us supposed to do?

BRAUKMANN. That bunch don't even want to work, they don't even want to.

SEIFFERT. But I want to, and I can't.

SLUPIANEK. The ending was a bit meagre, Seiffert, became a bit thin. Didn't exactly take our breath away. An exit like that usually gets tomatoes and rotten eggs. Mr Büscher, do you happen to have any pongy poultry products about your person?

BÜSCHER. I have had something: I've had a bellyful.

SLUPIANEK. But Mr Büscher, why are you sulking? Here stands Seiffert, star of the stage, and all you do is sulk. Doesn't he deserve a grander exit?

BÜSCHER. You make me throw up, Slupianek, that's all I've got to say, you make me throw up.

SLUPIANEK. Try giving us an encore, you pale imitation of Belmondo up there, speak. Up there, Monsieur Belmondo and down here, Herne's shittiest thickoes. Well. So that's all we're going to get, is it? Pitiful, really, pitiful. I've been reading a book, as well.

BÜSCHER. Slupianek's been reading a book, as well. Fancy me being among all these intellectuals.

SLUPIANEK. Button it, Büscher. This wasn't about caviare and boredom. This was about some really tough guys. Norwegians, they were. One fine day they said to themselves, easy as pie, we're going to conquer the South Pole. Up to then, no soul had ever set foot there, but they said, easy as pie, we're going to march to the Pole. Everyone just stood there with their mouths open, but they did it, they did it easy as pie.

BÜSCHER. Fairy-tale time. Here's the Moose in a noose, and you, Slupianek, tell us fairy-tales. Our Moose finds the Far North highly elevating, in fact, he's hung up on it from top to toe, and you witter on about the South Pole.

SLUPIANEK. What've you got against fairy-tales, Büscher?

BRAUKMANN. Right, Büscher, you're like a knife, forever cutting everything off.

SLUPIANEK. I'll meet you halfway, Seiffert, to show you I'm on your side. We cut out pinball and schnaps.

SEIFFERT. And then what?

SLUPIANEK. Then what?

SEIFFERT. Then what?

SLUPIANEK. Hm, then what? I've got an idea. How would it wash, Moose of Herne, how would you welcome something to do with the South Pole?

BÜSCHER. The penguins will be shocked rigid. Or don't they have them there?

SLUPIANEK. Right, let's stop chasing each other's tails. The Conquest of the South Pole by the Heroes of Herne. As a first step we shall see how I, Roald Amundsen, turn a geriatric moose into Mr Olaf Bjaaland, my comrade-in-arms against the everlasting ice. Let battle commence.

He grabs SEIFFERT. *The others release him from the noose.*

Scene Two: A Good Day

SLUPIANEK'*s room.*

SLUPIANEK (*reading*). The twenty-sixth of November dawned, a Sunday. It was a good day in more ways than one. I'd certainly had ample opportunity already to observe my comrades completing their trials, which gave me a rough idea what they were made of. But however long I live, I will never forget the trials they underwent on this particular day. During the night, the wind had veered back to the North and freshened to gale force. It was blowing and snowing so furiously that, as we emerged from our tent, we could hardly make out the sledges, which were all but covered in snow. The dogs had huddled together in a heap, trying their utmost to protect themselves against the blizzard. At minus twenty-seven degrees, the temperature was not in itself so terribly low, but it was low enough to be very unpleasant in blizzard conditions. One after the other, we all went outside to have a look at the weather, then we climbed into our sleeping bags and talked about how terrible our prospects were. Bloody awful weather, someone said. You could be forgiven for thinking it might never get any better. It's our fifth day today, and the blizzard's worse than ever. Yes, there was no disagreement about that. Then someone else said, nothing could be worse than having to lie in the same place in such appalling weather. More draining than marching all day long. I was of the same opinion. It might be quite pleasant, to lie still for a day, but for two, three, four or even – as now seemed likely – for five, no, that would be unbearable. Perhaps we should make another attempt at going on, someone said. As soon as this suggestion was put forward, it was carried with unanimous approbation. Whenever I recall those four friends who accompanied me on my expedition to the Pole, I often picture them as they were before me on that brilliant morning.

Scene Three (a): Force-feeding

BRAUKMANN'S *attic.*

SEIFFERT (*tied up on the floor*). I won't guzzle a morsel.

BRAUKMANN. He's being difficult.

BÜSCHER. Nice and easy now, we're going to get his grub-trap open, and Braukmann'll stuff it in. D'you want it in the major or minor?

SEIFFERT. Büscher, you scourge of humanity.

BÜSCHER. Right then, it's major. Serve away, chef.

BRAUKMANN. Jacket spuds.

BÜSCHER. Delish.

BRAUKMANN. One jacket spud for Büscher. One for Slupianek. And one for your dear old Braukmann.

BÜSCHER. Don't forget your Mattka. One more jacket spud for your Mattka. Where is she, by the way?

BRAUKMANN. Where d'you think? Work.

SEIFFERT. Work, don't let that word pass your lips, Braukmann, I beg you, don't let that word, work, pass your lips. Cut it out, or you'll find yourself having to stuff air into me, as well.

BÜSCHER. Don't vomit, Seiffert.

SLUPIANEK. Enough guzzling, enough wittering. Time to read. Braukmann, you read.

BRAUKMANN. Why me?

BÜSCHER. He's mislaid his spectacles.

BRAUKMANN. The same old tune. Play it again.

BÜSCHER. His specs, his specs, his specs he has mislaid.

BRAUKMANN. And this jacket spud, Seiffert.

LA BRAUKMANN, *with the washing.*

BÜSCHER. He spooned twelve eggs into him yesterday. Gave him such a hard-on, it shot through his trousers like a bolt from the blue.

SLUPIANEK. Naughty naughty.

BÜSCHER. Such a hard-on.

SLUPIANEK. There are ladies present.

LA BRAUKMANN. What's going on here?

BÜSCHER. Force-feeding H-block style.

LA BRAUKMANN. What's all this about, Braukmann? What's that bloke tied up for? What's the crockery doing here? I go out to work, while you –

BÜSCHER. Christ, Moose is holding his breath. Now he's holding his breath.

BRAUKMANN. Take that word back.

LA BRAUKMANN. I'm pissing myself.

BRAUKMANN. Plead with Seiffert.

LA BRAUKMANN. Brain having a day off?

BÜSCHER. Ambulance.

BRAUKMANN. He's already gone blue all over.

LA BRAUKMANN. Why's he holding his breath? What's it all about?

SLUPIANEK. Explanations later, madam. Tickle the Moose. Dig him in the ribs.

BRAUKMANN. He's breathing. He's laughing.

BÜSCHER. There you are laughing, see. That's got you laughing all right. There's plenty to laugh about, friends, let's all have a laugh. There's plenty to laugh about. Yes, today's laughter day.

LA BRAUKMANN. No, today's laundry day.

The men go out.

Braukmann, you stay.

LA BRAUKMANN *hangs up the washing line that* SEIFFERT *was tied up with.*

Scene 3(b): Hanging Out the Washing

LA BRAUKMANN. I've had enough, Braukmann, I've had enough. Pinball, schnaps, the end. Monkey business in the attic. Who knows what's next? He's sunk to new depths, that's what he's sunk to, new depths. You shudder to think, that's what you shudder to do, think. It's enough to make your blood run cold, your blood run cold is what it's enough to make. When it comes to monkey business, Braukmann is a star. He gives his all. As long as he's acting the fool. Then he can dance. Then he can laugh. Then he's got something to laugh about. But the rest of the time – There he sits, gnawing his nails. There he glares, if you dare to talk to him. There are his moods. Being unemployed just isn't fair, he can't bear it. It's so bloody unfair he can't get his arse off the chair any more, can't speak for despair. There he is suffering. There he is, being Gandhi. But any chance of monkey business and he's raring to go. Never a care. There he's got flair. I've had enough, Braukmann, I've had enough.

BRAUKMANN *goes out.*

When we were kids we always used to play Stay-where-you-are-and-don't-move-a-muscle. When Mother came up the creaky old stairs, we made ourselves scarce. The attic was out of bounds. Up here was the only place the coal dust couldn't blow about as it did below. And Mother was constantly washing. Constantly washing and wiping. Always up and at it. Father's things in particular she was constantly washing. She'd stuck a postcard behind the mirror. There was a mountain on it, covered with ice and snow. White, everything white, she once said, chance would be a fine thing. The washing and wiping I inherited. Grease is what I'm up against. Given the choice between hairdressing and chip-frying, I said to myself, I'd rather touch greasy chips than greasy chaps. Now I'm up to my eye-balls in grease. But I picked up a trick from a film. Get back from work, strip off, rub myself all over with a hefty chunk of lemon. The bird in the film sold fish not chips, but fish or fat it still does the trick. I'm for films. But I can't ever get Braukmann to go to the cinema. The one time I did, the film was about a bloke who was unemployed, and before you could blink, he was off. He won't face it, he can't face it. Sometimes he just sits at the table cowering, and stares at the wall. Just sits there cowering and stares at the wall. Bad, really bad. I can't help him. And he just sits there cowering and stares at the wall.

Scene Four: Further Education

The attic.

BÜSCHER. There's washing hanging on the line.

BRAUKMANN. For crying out loud, still here?

BÜSCHER. It's dry as a bone.

BRAUKMANN. Paws off.

BÜSCHER. I thought we could do anything up here. I thought, now we've got through the whole book, we could do anything up here.

BRAUKMANN. Not with washing hanging on the line.

BÜSCHER. You wanna watch Slupianek doesn't hang you.

BRAUKMANN. It's not my fault washing's hanging on the line.

BÜSCHER. Here he comes. No, it's Seiffert.

SEIFFERT. What a nuisance.

BRAUKMANN. What?

SEIFFERT. The washing's hanging on the line.

BRAUKMANN. Yes, the washing's hanging on the line.

SEIFFERT. What can we do?

BÜSCHER. There's nothing we can do.

SEIFFERT. Pathetic, Braukmann, really pathetic. We should get going. Where's Slupianek? What will Slupianek say?

BÜSCHER. Slupianek's spitting hemlock and wormwood.

SEIFFERT. I nearly blew a gasket getting here, getting here I nearly blew a gasket.

BÜSCHER. And I left my floosie high and dry. Come, she said. I said, tomorrow. Today, she said. I said, no go. Oh, another bird, she said. Bollocks, I said. What is it then, say what it is, she said. I won't say, I said. She said, you've gotta say. I said, South Pole, and that's all I am saying. She said, you're only saying that. I said, stop it, it's the truth. She said, if you say so. I said, I do say so. Yes, friends, I escape a row by the skin of my scrotum, and here washing's hanging on the line.

SEIFFERT. The boss.

BÜSCHER. Braukmann, make for cover. Slupianek, what do you say to that?

SLUPIANEK. White, everything white.

SEIFFERT. What's the matter with him?

SLUPIANEK. Never before, friends, have I set eyes on a more beautiful, wilder landscape. Such massive blocks of ice frozen solid. A mountain range to the left. Crazy outlines of the mountains. Waves of ice, compacted. Between the perilous chasms ice finials and icicles. Everything white, everything a whirring white.

SEIFFERT. Excuse me, Slupianek, that sheet there.

SLUPIANEK. A glacier, Seiffert, a magnificent glacier. Never before, friends, has any human being set foot on this whacking great deluge of cracking ice. We're going to be the first.

BRAUKMANN. The washing has no part in it, Slupianek.

SEIFFERT. And what does this represent?

SLUPIANEK. Well, friends, it's the notorious Hell's Gates.

BÜSCHER. With a remote resemblance to Braukmann's underpants.

SLUPIANEK. Well, you'll need to stretch your imagination.

BRAUKMANN. Let's get going, friends. Once my Mattka comes back, she'll clear it all away, and we'll have the whole place to ourselves.

SLUPIANEK. Are you out of your mind, Braukmann? No one lays a finger on a single stitch.

SEIFFERT. He means it, you Oliver Cromwell.

BRAUKMANN. That's enough, Slupianek. I can hear footsteps.

SLUPIANEK. We'll do a deal.

BRAUKMANN. She'll throw us out on our arses, on our arses.

SLUPIANEK. Who knows? Praps she'd join the group and leave the landscape as it is.

BÜSCHER. Come in on the expedition as our fifth man.

SLUPIANEK. Nice one, Büscher.

BÜSCHER. You've already got up my nose, wanting to cut one out.

SLUPIANEK. Not wanting to, having to. In our corps we've no more than four.

BRAUKMANN. She'll never join in anyway, never.

SLUPIANEK. Try.

BRAUKMANN. She'll stone me to death.

SLUPIANEK. Then I'll get you out of the line of fire, Braukmann, I'll take the flak. You're already tied up tonight.

BRAUKMANN. What am I?

SLUPIANEK. I've enrolled you. You're on a cookery course.

BRAUKMANN. Cookery course.

BÜSCHER. Lucky you.

BRAUKMANN. Why a cookery course?

SLUPIANEK. He is wise who looks ahead. And I, Braukmann, have looked ahead. Here's your enrolment form. And you'd better get a move on. As it happens, you'll be able to go a partlet of the way with Büscher. He's got to go to the Ruhr Park.

BÜSCHER. Interesting. What am I doing there?

SLUPIANEK. You've got to suss this out under cover of darkness.

BÜSCHER. The Eskimo shop. I've always wanted to go there.

SLUPIANEK. I read your every desire in your eyes.

SEIFFERT. Well, what I'd like to know now is what my desire is.

SLUPIANEK. Your desire, Seiffert, has for a long time been to study the husky at close quarters. Gelsenkirchen has some splendid specimens.

SEIFFERT. Got a ticket for the zoo?

SLUPIANEK. It's free on Wednesdays. UB40s half-price.

SEIFFERT. And the fare, boss.

SLUPIANEK. Fare-dodging sharpens the wits. Let's get weaving, friends. I'll hold the fort.

BRAUKMANN. You're guarding a lost position, Slupianek.

BÜSCHER. I bet you, before you've even said – 'Evening – , your mountain range is about to be ironed, and your waves of ice are about to be flattened by the mangle.

SLUPIANEK. Let's wait and see.

BRAUKMANN. And why can't I do the dogs?

SLUPIANEK. Never do anything haphazardly, Braukmann. Always work methodically. Explanations later.

BÜSCHER (*pulls* FRANKIEBOY *out of his hiding place*). Take Frankieboy along with you, Seiffert, take him along with you. He's got a soft spot for animals.

BRAUKMANN. Specially monkeys, huh.

BÜSCHER. One more word from you, Braukmann.

SLUPIANEK. Right. Suss out the dogs, Frankieboy, suss them out.

BÜSCHER. Nice one, Slupianek, nice one.

SLUPIANEK. Praps he can join the group. Frankieboy, give us a bark.

FRANKIEBOY. Bow-wow.

SLUPIANEK. Well done, Frankieboy. Well barked.

SEIFFERT. Frankieboy does that well.

BÜSCHER. How about him, Slupianek, as our fifth man?

SLUPIANEK. Don't get carried away, Büscher.

SEIFFERT. Frankieboy, don't make me grin.

BÜSCHER. Grin, Seiffert, grin. And I'll grin back.

BRAUKMANN. Right, Büscher.

SLUPIANEK. Frankieboy, sing us 'Strangers in the Night'. D'you want to?

BÜSCHER. No he doesn't.

SLUPIANEK. You always like 'Strangers in the Night'.

BÜSCHER. Don't sing, Frankie.

FRANKIEBOY (*stuttering*). Why shouldn't Frankieboy?

BÜSCHER. It's okay by me. If any one of you pulls a face, that'll set the cat among the pigeons.

SLUPIANEK. Over to you.

FRANKIEBOY (*sings*). Strangers in the Night –

BÜSCHER. That'll do. Nicely sung, Frankie, nice.

SEIFFERT. Funny. He usually stutters.

BRAUKMANN. Footsteps, I can hear footsteps.

BÜSCHER. Out through the skylight. Slupianek, never say die.

Scene Five: Lottery

SLUPIANEK. Whilst Braukmann is attending his cookery course, he, Slupianek, wrestles with her, La Braukmann, about the washing staying in the attic. In this struggle he is determined to use any means fair or foul, provided they lead to success; and he is convinced that he will win this battle, if only he's prepared to fling himself wholeheartedly into the fray, even if this means asking her, La Braukmann, whether she's on the pill. And he does.

LA BRAUKMANN. She asks him, if he, Slupianek, could imagine sleeping with her even without any kind of contraceptive precautions. No one could, or for that matter should, foresee what else might be released in her, in him, in both of them, if they slept together. The after-effects might be far-reaching, she supposes, and against them the coil and the condom would both be useless. All this was beside the point, because in any case she didn't use any form of contraception, on the contrary, she grabbed every chance to have a child, because an accident when she was younger had made it nearly impossible for her to conceive. But, she stresses the nearly. Even if there isn't much of a chance, it does still exist, and so she must, as she was sure he would understand, take advantage of every opportunity. It's like a lottery, she adds, as an afterthought.

SLUPIANEK. He, Slupianek, is confused by this explanation, and the word lottery reverberates inside his skull like a tombola on a TV game show. On the one hand there is the washing, which is still in the attic, and had to stay there, and on the other there was what had just been said.

LA BRAUKMANN. She is aware of his turmoil.

SLUPIANEK. A lottery, he thinks. No, he says, under his breath, but as she had pressed her ear close to his mouth she could hear it distinctly.

LA BRAUKMANN. Forget I said that, she says, forget it.

SLUPIANEK. He gives her no clues, either by word or by gesture, whether he wanted to or could forget.

LA BRAUKMANN. Because of her great yearning for a child, she doesn't try to get any deeper into him, but hopes he will into her.

SLUPIANEK. His body senses her closeness, her warmth, and he presses up against her.

LA BRAUKMANN. But before she surrenders to the impulse of their bodies she takes one more little look at the washing that's in front of her, the washing in the attic, that is dry and ought by rights to be taken down.

Scene Six: The Break-in

Eskimo shop at night.

BÜSCHER. Self-service, gents.

SLUPIANEK. All needs supplied. Furs. Tents. Snow goggles. Ice-picks.

BRAUKMANN. A man.

SEIFFERT. Bollocks, a shadow.

SLUPIANEK. I have.

BÜSCHER. We have.

SLUPIANEK. Has Braukmann?

SEIFFERT. Empty hands is what Braukmann has. They're shaking as if he's feverish.

BRAUKMANN. I can't do it.

SEIFFERT. He's backing out.

SLUPIANEK. What's his trouble?

SEIFFERT. He can't do it. He's backing out.

BRAUKMANN. I have kept it from you, since yesterday I've had a job.

BÜSCHER. What is it he has?

SEIFFERT. A job.

BRAUKMANN. Are you telling me to risk everything?

SLUPIANEK. Yes, but on our game.
          First side with us.
          Get tried with us.
          Then die with us.

Packs up the things for BRAUKMANN.

Scene Seven: Wisting, or a Polar Bear

Outside BRAUKMANN's *house.*

SLUPIANEK. Knocked off already, Braukmann. Or may I call you Wisting? Oscar Wisting, Petty Officer in the Marines?

SEIFFERT. He's not all that happy, our Braukmann, even though he's on his way back from work.

SLUPIANEK. Praps he took a cut in wages to get the job.

BÜSCHER. Course he took a cut in wages to get the job.

SLUPIANEK. Praps he said he'd work through the holidays.

BÜSCHER. Course he said he'd work through the holidays.

SLUPIANEK. And who knows what else?

BRAUKMANN. Let me past, friends.

BÜSCHER. Back home to Mattka.

BRAUKMANN. Let me through.

SLUPIANEK. Watch out. Can't you see: hole upon hole, crack upon crack, crevasse upon crevasse? Vast blocks of ice in between. A crack opens up like a gun going off. Snow billows up. The ice cracks kilometres wide. Roar after roar, echoing. Another gun going off. Fountains of snow, sky high. Chaos, white chaos. The rearing head of a polar bear, in between, sniffing. Got my gun. Here she is. Loaded.

BÜSCHER. Hang on – whatever it is standing there grinning like a snow-king is not a bear. No, it's Wisting. It is Wisting, is it not?

SLUPIANEK. Is it Wisting, or a polar bear?

SEIFFERT. Not a peep. Shoot, shoot, that is not Wisting.

BÜSCHER. Its expression is inscrutable.

SLUPIANEK. Then it must be a polar bear.

BÜSCHER. Polar bear, or Wisting.

SLUPIANEK. Rear notch and front sight.

BRAUKMANN. No, it's me, your Wisting.

SEIFFERT. It is him.

SLUPIANEK. Oh God, that's a relief.

BÜSCHER. It's him, our Wisting.

SLUPIANEK.⎤   Can a camel ride a bike?
BÜSCHER. ⎥   No, no, no.
SEIFFERT. ⎦   Why not?
            Course not.
            Because, because, because –

BRAUKMANN. He's go no thumb to ring the bell.

SLUPIANEK. And as it's you, Wisting, we can go on. Bjaaland, the moose, will lead the way.

BÜSCHER. That's his strong point.

SEIFFERT. As if on an invisible rope. Don't waver by a metre. Hold the course. Straight ahead. Straight ahead. Do I wander off to the right? No. Or to the left? On no account. Straight ahead, straight ahead. What can I look at without getting dizzy? Is that a hill over there? No, just a whirr of snow.

SLUPIANEK. Well walked, Bjaaland. We can pitch camp. The tent.

BÜSCHER. Where are we, Amundsen?

SLUPIANEK. Later on, we'll call it the Butcher's Shop.

BÜSCHER. The Butcher's Shop, why?

SLUPIANEK. I said, later.

SEIFFERT. Now what? I can't hear anything, Wisting.

BRAUKMANN. Draw your rations. Wisting revealed an outstanding talent for cooking. He put pemmican cakes, which contained more herbs than anything else, into a soup, and in a jiffy served us a delicious meat-broth with vegetables. But the highpoint of the meal was the second course. Even if we had doubts about the quality of the meat, they were dispelled immediately we tasted it. The meat was superb, and at lightning speed one little spare rib disappeared after another. However, I must admit: despite its quality, it could have been a fraction more tender. But you can't expect miracles from dog meat.

SLUPIANEK. It was a great effort to find a suitable site on which to pitch camp; the snow was frozen so hard. Eventually, we found one, and erected the tent as usual. That evening, we lit the primus stove with unaccustomed haste, and went on pumping it until the air pressure gauge read maximum. I was hoping by this means to make as much noise as possible, so as to drown the noise of the shots, which were soon to go off outside. Twenty-four of our most hard-working comrades and most loyal assistants were to suffer death. It was hard, but it had to happen. We needed their meat for ourselves and for the remaining dogs.

BÜSCHER (*he pulls* FRANKIEBOY *out of his hiding-place*). Including Lasse, my favourite.

SLUPIANEK. Including Lasse. Now the first shot rang out. I'm not usually nervous, but I must admit it gave me a shock. Then came shot after shot - unnervingly they rang out throughout the vast wasteland.

BRAUKMANN (*looks at his watch*). For crying out loud! I'm for the high jump.

BÜSCHER. Hell's Gates as well.

BRAUKMANN. For Christ's sake, my Mattka.

SEIFFERT. Don't be a frog, stop croaking. In this weather we can manage a few more kilometrelets.

SLUPIANEK. The wind's dying down, and it's not coming from the East any more.

BÜSCHER. Right, Hell's Gates as well.

BRAUKMANN. Hell's Gates, may I have the pleasure? Who is first?

SLUPIANEK. The Moose is first. And why, Braukmann?

BRAUKMANN. At the notorious Hell's Gates, Bjaaland and his team suddenly fell through a treacherous bridge of snow and were left hanging over the chasm. Hanssen shouted to Bjaaland, who was clinging to his sledge: Hang on, Bjaaland, I'll just get the photographic apparatus. Amundsen shouted: What does the crevasse look like, and Bjaaland calmly answered from below: Oh, what you'd expect, bottomless.

SLUPIANEK. Well done, Braukmann. Your go, Seiffert, your go.

SEIFFERT *goes through Hell's Gates, followed by* BÜSCHER, SLUPIANEK *and* FRANKIEBOY.

BRAUKMANN (*in front of Hell's Gates*). What exactly is pemmican?

SLUPIANEK. Well asked, Braukmann, well asked. Here's the recipe. Wisting, our kitchen genius, you produce some for us as your homework.

BRAUKMANN. You take –

Scene Eight: Pigeons

Pigeon-loft at SLUPIANEK's.

LA BRAUKMANN. Would you show me your pigeons, Slupianek? You have got some, haven't you?

SLUPIANEK. One has some, one has some.

LA BRAUKMANN. Lots, Slupianek.

SLUPIANEK. Forty. Praps more, praps less.

LA BRAUKMANN. One can afford to be generous.

SLUPIANEK. In my Father's day there were forty. He left them to me. And this loft is his work too, his life's work. A miner's pride and joy – pigeons. And I keep them out of respect for him. A pal without pigeons is like a bog without a bum. His very words.

LA BRAUKMANN. His very words.

SLUPIANEK. That's right. What is one after?

LA BRAUKMANN. Slupianek, let Braukmann be. He has a job, has a family, has a child.

SLUPIANEK. Child?

LA BRAUKMANN. Here.

SLUPIANEK. Lucky blighter, old Braukmann. He's really come up trumps. Scored a hat-trick. Congratulations.

LA BRAUKMANN. That's enough fooling and faffing about, Slupianek, call it a day. Let Braukmann be. The child needs a father. South Pole.

SLUPIANEK. Listen to my ladies cooing. This one's Frances, my favourite. Paola. Nicola. And and and – I am Casanova.

LA BRAUKMANN. You're a pushover, Slupianek. No brains. No bread. Stick to your pigeons, they do at least coo. Who would want you?

SLUPIANEK. Probly you, my sweet little pie. You've been defused. Skimpily clad and well stacked. Good to grope. Cosmetics and trinkets, what's it all about?

LA BRAUKMANN. Get yourself a steady, Slupianek, show a bit of sense.

SLUPIANEK. I'm a born individualist, my sweet little pie. Always drawn the line at slippers on my feet and spots on my face. Praps a capful of kids, you know me.

LA BRAUKMANN. Only too well.

SLUPIANEK. Dance with me, my sweet little pie, forget Braukmann for a few steps.

LA BRAUKMANN. Slupianek, the great South Pole explorer in the fridge, the perfect pal in the everlasting ice. Ice-cold, that's what you are, Slupianek, ice-cold.

SLUPIANEK. Have a schnaps, that'll warm you up.

LA BRAUKMANN. Nothing but booze, make-believe and blarney. Sod off to the South Pole.

SLUPIANEK (*sings*). I want to say ta
　　　　　　For that shining star
　　　　　　Over Herne afar.

LA BRAUKMANN. Hands off my washing.

SLUPIANEK. Let me lead you astray, my sweet little pie, or I'll lead him further astray.

LA BRAUKMANN (*drawing a pistol*). Then I'll take a shot at you.

SLUPIANEK. Annie's got her gun. But I know that shooter. It's only a toy, love.

LA BRAUKMANN. For the last time, let Braukmann get on with it.

SLUPIANEK. If you'll let me get on with it. Bang, bang. Load it, little lady. First tipple, then tinkle.

LA BRAUKMANN. It's loaded. What now?

A shot

SLUPIANEK. The gun –

LA BRAUKMANN. – has got what it takes. Now, Slupianek, let's stop chasing each other's tails. I say, that's enough of Braukmann and the South Pole. I say, he's my husband. I say he's the father of the child. I say, Braukmann has a job, and he needs it, we need it.

SLUPIANEK. Tell Daddy Braukmann. Why me?

LA BRAUKMANN. Because you're always at the bottom of everything that makes my life
stink. Braukmann's lost his marbles. Stands over the stove secretly at dead of night. It stinks
to high heaven. He can't open his eyes in the morning and staggers off to work like a
zombie. In his free time he slips out of my grasp. I find junk behind the wardrobe. Covered
in Eskimo-shop labels. I read in the paper about a break-in. Stealing his way to the South
Pole, Slupianek. What's Braukmann up to on his nightshift by the stove? What does he
need the furs and picks for? Right then, Slupianek, if you're such a keen dancer, let's do the
last tango of Herne.

SLUPIANEK. Leave the shooter alone.

LA BRAUKMANN. Leave Braukmann alone.

SLUPIANEK. Over my dead body. Shoot me here, through the heart. I'll die in delight, in
sight of Herne. Come on, shoot me, my sweet little pie.

LA BRAUKMANN. Not you, your pigeons.

Shoots at the pigeons.

Scene Nine: Change of Programme

The attic. BRAUKMANN *at the stove.* SEIFFERT *on his knees re-painting a Norwegian flag.*
BÜSCHER. FRANKIEBOY.

SLUPIANEK (*coming in*). All present. All prepared.

BRAUKMANN. For Christ's sake, my heart missed a beat. I thought . . . my Mattka.

SLUPIANEK. No reason to panic. I sneaked past her stall, she's doing a roaring trade.
Today's guzzling day. We're safe.

BRAUKMANN. The way you handled the washing business. Speechless and Sons is all I can
say. It was hanging for three days, three whole days.

SLUPIANEK. We aim to give satisfaction.

BRAUKMANN. Hats off to Slupianek, hats off. How did you handle it?

SLUPIANEK. Trade secret, Wisting, just like your recipe. Pemmican, delish. Dynorods your
tubes.

BRAUKMANN. Yup, he's certainly got a lot up top, our Amundsen.

SLUPIANEK (*beginning to erect a tent*). Seiffert's song, two three.

SEIFFERT
BRAUKMANN } (*singing*). Amundsen, our navigator
SLUPIANEK   Through everlasting ice and snow,
> First he had a moose in a noose,
> Then he was in the know.
> Bjaaland struts like a street-walker,
> Straight ahead with a confident air,
> A crevasse to the right,
> A crevasse to the left,
> But he never turns a hair.
>
> It's Wisting our kitchen genius
> Who cooks us pemmican,
> And serves up hot huskies which we
> First shot down with a gun.

> Lasse is harnessed up by Hanssen
> They both bolt off towards the Pole
> As the great Hell's Gates roar,
> Now behind now before
> He's a very happy soul.

BÜSCHER. I've been thumbing through the preface. The preface often turns out to be my favourite part of a book.

BRAUKMANN. Yeah, that's where you find all the answers.

BÜSCHER. Absolutely, Braukmann, or Wisting, or whatever your name is. Right then. I've been thumbing through the preface, the preface which you, Slupianek, have kept from us.

SEIFFERT. So you've been thumbing through the preface, have you? Did you all get that? He's been thumbing through the preface.

BÜSCHER. You've got it, Seiffert, I've been thumbing through the preface. And while I'm thumbing through the preface I find out there is a very different story, which has much more crust and crumb. It's crunchy on the inside as well, Slupianek, not as slick as Amundsen's. So as I am thumbing through the preface –

SEIFFERT. As Büscher is thumbing through the preface –

BRAUKMANN. As I am thumbing through the preface –

BRAUKMANN. What's it all about, Büscher? Büscher, what's it all about?

SLUPIANEK. Who answers to the name of Büscher round here? I don't know any Büscher. I only know Ice Pilot Mr Helmer Hanssen, Customs Officer in civilian life, I know him.

SEIFFERT. Customs Officer in civilian life.

SLUPIANEK. Well, Mr Helmer Hanssen, what caught your eye as you were thumbing through the preface?

BÜSCHER. As I, Büscher, a UB40 in civilian life, am thumbing through the preface, I find out there are four men called Shackleton, Adams, Marshall and Wild, funnily enough there are four of them just like us, we don't have to cut anyone out, like we did with the Norwegians, so as I am thumbing through the preface, Slupianek, I find out these four take a more brilliant line than Amundsen and Co.

BRAUKMANN. You don't say, Büscher.

BÜSCHER. But I do say, Braukmann. They didn't go hell-for-leather to the Pole, hello there, here we are.

SEIFFERT. How did they then, tell on.

BRAUKMANN. How did they?

BÜSCHER. How, how? They used ponies instead of dogs –

SLUPIANEK. Which was totally wrong-headed and disastrous.

BÜSCHER. I'll say. They never potted the Pole. Too true. They were, however, finished before they got to the finish, and now I'll read. On the ninth of January, 1909 at nine o'clock in the morning, after a brisk march, we reached latitude 88 degrees 23 minutes south. Following the last blizzard the way ahead was frozen solid. We pointed the binoculars to the south, but all we could see in every direction was the interminable white expanse of snow. Nowhere on this plain, which extended all the way to the Pole, could we make out any variation, but we know, the goal that we haven't yet reached, lies on this plain. We don't linger long in this position, but roll up the flag, turn round and set out on our return journey. So we are now going back on our tracks. However disappointed we are, we have the consolation of having done everything in our power.

SLUPIANEK. Why are you faffing on about this failure?

BÜSCHER. You call it that, Benno. For me it's what keeps the whole thing going. So they don't say: right then, that's that, gentlemen. That doesn't appeal to me at all, Benno. And because I'm more interested in failures, I'll give out new parts. So Braukmann should be Shackleton, he shouldn't only cook pemmican, but he should also be Shackleton. And the rest of us – Seiffert, you give out the parts – Adams, Marshall and Wild.

SLUPIANEK. You've got a nasty way of putting things, Büscher, you've got a nasty way of putting things.

BRAUKMANN. Right, Büscher.

BÜSCHER. I'm giving back the part you gave me so grandly, Benno. I'm giving it back to you, and I wish the others would follow suit.

SLUPIANEK. You're a highly negative character, Büscher, as we know. Your sort always come crawling back, begging: You take over, I can't cope. So you play Mr Robert F. Scott, our rival in the race. We'll play the tortoises, but we'll get there, while Hare comes to grief in a terrifying snowstorm lasting nine days, before rolling over with his paws in the air.

BÜSCHER. The hindmost dog may catch the hare, Slupianek, am I on about suicide?

SLUPIANEK. But Büscher, why settle for the booby prize when we can go for the jackpot?

BRAUKMANN. Right, Büscher.

SLUPIANEK. Do you want to chuck away the moment of realisation, we've done it, the Conquest of the South Pole. Do you want to chuck away our success of the fourteenth of December, 1911? What will people say? After our celebration meal – a magnificent joint of seal – our joy reached new heights when Bjaaland took out a full cigar case and passed it round. A cigar at the Pole. Nothing could beat that.

BÜSCHER. I know that silvery voice of yours. Go to Hamelin, ratcatcher. There are no rats here. Are there?

SLUPIANEK. You're standing on the hose, Büscher, and even if an elephant were standing on the hose, I'd shave its feet.

BÜSCHER. Cheeky, Slupianek.

SLUPIANEK. And you're bloody-minded. He's after a failure. I'm after a triumph.

BÜSCHER. No, it's not triumphs we need to act out, friends, not triumphs. We do failures better, they're our staple diet. Every trip to the jobcentre is a failure. Every phone call about a job ad is a failure. Opening so many doors you polish the knobs. Every refusal, a failure. And Braukmann, even your work, even that is just a failure. A paid failure, a badly paid one. Human beings are just one big failure. And so the failure must go on and on for ever and ever, a hundred times, a thousand times until we're all sick to death. It's only when you're up to your eyes in shit, desperately gasping for air, and the thinnest current of air is getting thinner and thinner, when you're really on your last legs, then the vomit might rise so high in your throat that you lash out mercilessly in all directions. Then, Slupianek, we wouldn't just be shooting a few dogs, we'd be letting fly at anyone who got at us, or stood on our hose. It's not lucky old Amundsen we must be, but unlucky old Shackleton. For Christ's sake, Seiffert, our moose, Braukmann, our pelican cook, our Gandhi. Benno, join me. We are Shackleton, Adams, Marshall and Wild. Poor buggers who can see their goal somewhere ahead of them, however hazily. It's in the distance, in the whiteness, in the glimmering, in the ice, in the coldness. In the distance, that's where it is.

BRAUKMANN. What's up with him?

SEIFFERT. He's hollering.

BRAUKMANN. For Christ's sake, Büscher's hollering.

SEIFFERT. What sort of guys were they?

BÜSCHER. They were Brits.

SLUPIANEK. What are you up to, Mr Olaf Bjaaland? What are you up to?

SEIFFERT. I'm repainting the flag. It's turning out all right.

SLUPIANEK (*at the door*). I'll not change course, lads, but leave you behind,
    You boring bunch, one day on top of the world,
    The next down in the dumps. Three bobble caps
    Red noses below stamping through the snow
    Frost-blooms on your bums, icicles on your cocks.
    Look, Büscher, look you dwarf, Seiffert, you worm.
    Flag-defacer, and sex-cripple Braukmann.
    I set my compass for the South, with a cheery
    Goodbye wave to 88, 23.
    I've had more than my fair share of failure, lads,
    For long enough, I don't need any more.
    And now, as a farewell to my dwarf gents,
    How would you like a little snowball fight?
    Not got the guts even for that. I'll piddle
    A southwards course for you through the snow, perhaps
    There'll be someone there with so much moral strength
    He won't just want to be rooted to this spot.

SLUPIANEK *goes off.*

Scene Ten: The South Pole Child

SLUPIANEK'*s room.*

SLUPIANEK. Four legs are needed for chairs, yes, understood.
    But why four? Who says it must be four? Why four?
    I won't have it. Seems a bit too many.
    The saw, then. I'll cut three off. Then perhaps
    We'll find mankind has made a big mistake.
    Four are uncalled for. Four are three too many.
    Let's root out the weeds. Long live the lone leg.
    Sole soldier wooden leg. Freedom fighter crutch.
    The saw, then. Turn four into one. I'll have
    Nothing in my room to do with four.
    The saw, then.

Saws, and cuts himself.

Not my idea of fun. Now I'm bleeding. Bleeding like a pig. Now I'm bleeding piglike. But why a pig? Who mentioned pigs? I am Amundsen, the South Pole traveller.

Drinks.

Christ lads, it's got to come out in the open, that Slupianek, Benno, unmarried, unemployed, is all done in. All done in he is. He's finished, once and for all. Flat out, smashed. Beating about the bush won't do any good. He is dead beat, bushed and dead beat. All he can do is put his paws in the air. Pick up his hat and go. He's got nothing more to say for himself. Exit. He's completely broken down, broken down in the ice. The drive-belt's given way. The tip of the flag-pole. He hasn't got a chance any more, he's had all his chances. Man overboard. SLUPIANEK, THE GREAT SOUTH POLE TRAVELLER IN THE FRIDGE. I can't even see a fridge. Have I gone snowblind? For crying out loud, I'm finished. Covered in crap up to my cranium. Done in. Finished. Put an end to it.

Drinks.

Hang on. There is something, after all. There is something. And it isn't after all so little. After all, something really vital has been overlooked, after all. It's a child. After all, a child won in a lottery. The jackpot. I'm a millionaire, after all. Count Coke from Herne. Christ Almighty, a child in Christ. I'm getting hot, hot's what I'm getting. The top of my skull is lifting off. For Christ's sake, a child. It'll be a snowchild. The first snowbody will now become somebody. A child. It's already on a journey. Amundsen, harness the dogs. Mustn't miss this first night, featuring the first child's cry at the South Pole. It must have a name then. Hold on, I've got it. Antarcticus. Or Antarctica, course. The South Pole child. Conceived on the journey, born at the goal. It's already clambering out of its cot. A sealskin, course. It plants its feet on ice and snow. Then we'll go for a spin with the huskies. Criss-crossing the landscape. To mark the occasion, the penguins all wear tails. A polar bear grins. We have a snowball-fight. And when we're ravenous at night we'll polish off half a seal. The South Pole child, that was the cue.

Drinks.

> Then you'll trace your course. The globe's now too small.
> From the South to the North Pole – just one small step.
> You've still got your heel in the Bay of Whales
> While stubbing your big toe on the Himalayas.
> Beneath your feet you can feel desert sand.
> The wide sea glints a foot's breadth away
> Around your little toe schools of dolphins play.

Scene Eleven: Braukmann's Dream

The BRAUKMANNs' *kitchen. Night.*

BRAUKMANN. Shackleton. Here it is. In the whole history of the world, there will probably never be a clearer testimony to what a human being can achieve when he exerts all his strength and willpower. Shackleton's great exploit is one of the most inspiring chapters in the history of Antarctic exploration. Latitude 88 degrees, 23 minutes south. If it's 88 degrees, 23 minutes, and one degree equals sixty minutes, altogether that's 97 minutes short of the Pole. One degree equals 111 kilometres. So, 60 minutes into 111 kilometres – 60 into 111, that makes, that makes, that –

Nods off, dreams.

LEFTRIGHTLEFTRIGHTLEFTANDRIGHT THE GREAT SHACKLETON'S IN SIGHT

THE GREAT SHACKLETON THE GREAT MANOMETER KILOMETRE

PLEASE PLEASE PLEASE DEAR DOCTOR ERWIN MOOSE

NINETY MINUS EIGHTY-EIGHT TWENTY-THREE EQUALS NINETY-SEVEN ONE HUNDRED AND ELEVEN DIVIDED BY SIXTY EQUALS ONE POINT EIGHT FIVE ACCORDING TO ISAAC NEWTON NINETY-SEVEN MULTIPLIED BY ONE POINT EIGHT FIVE MAKES ONE HUNDRED AND SEVENTY-NINE POINT FOUR FIVE

A PLACE IN THE HISTORY BOOKS

WHY A PLACE IN THE HISTORY BOOKS GAVE IN ONE HUNDRED AND SEVENTY-NINE SHORT OF THE GOAL

IT DOESN'T DETRACT FROM KING SHACKLETON

KILOMETRE-LONG FISSURES IN THE ICE

NIGGLER

THE SNOW-KING REJECTS DOGS RELIES ON PONIES

NIGGLER NIGGLING

REASONS FOR REASONS

DOWN WITH NIGGLERS HURRAH FOR SHACKLETON HURRAH

ONE HUNDRED AND SEVENTY-NINE POINT FOUR FIVE

LA BRAUKMANN. Braukmann. What are you doing on the table, Braukmann? What are you doing on the kitchen table at this hour of the night? Here we go again. It's back to monkey business. Your bum's hanging out of your trousers, but you're whistling La Paloma.

BRAUKMANN. It was only a dream, nothing more.

LA BRAUKMANN. A dream.

BRAUKMANN. A dream, what else?

LA BRAUKMANN. Braukmann, am I dreaming, am I awake, am I alive, am I conscious? Braukmann, tell me, am I dreaming, if I see a book there, am I dreaming there is a book there, that wasn't there yesterday, am I dreaming? Is there a book there or not, tell me, Braukmann? And on that book are there clear letters which spell the words South Pole, or aren't there, or is no book there at all, or am I just dreaming?

BRAUKMANN. There certainly is a book there, but it's as if it wasn't there.

LA BRAUKMANN. Magic spells, Braukmann. It's not just a buffoon getting up to monkey business I have here, not just a sleep-dancer, I've also got a magician here. Spells, Braukmann. Cut out the spells. Sit down. I want to know right now where I stand. The child needs a father. What I need is beside the point. But the child needs a father. Not a buffoon. Not a sleep-dancer. Not a magician. Are we agreed?

BRAUKMANN. Of course.

LA BRAUKMANN. What's happening with the South Pole?

BRAUKMANN. It's been South Pole-axed.

LA BRAUKMANN. Think I'll believe it?

BRAUKMANN. You should believe it.

LA BRAUKMANN. That's the end of it.

BRAUKMANN. It's the end of that.

LA BRAUKMANN. You've called the whole thing off.

BRAUKMANN. They were great times.

LA BRAUKMANN. Were.

BRAUKMANN. Were.

They put their arms round each other.

BRAUKMANN. Tell me, does 97 times 1.85 make 179.45?

LA BRAUKMANN. Get into bed. By five in the morning, the night's over.

BRAUKMANN. No, honestly, is it 179.45?

LA BRAUKMANN. Of course, of course.

BRAUKMANN. So it is 179.45.

Scene Twelve (a): Birthday

The BRAUKMANNS' *front room.* LA BRAUKMANN, BRAUKMANN, BÜSCHER, SEIFFERT, RUDI *and* ROSI.

ROSI (*smoking, to the audience*). I'm Rosi, the divorcee. Funny, isn't it. They call me Rosi the divorcee here. Not just plain Rosi – no, Rosi the divorcee. Alexander the Great, Ivan the Terrible, Rosi the divorcee. Before that, they called me Rosi the cherry-stone. My ex always called me Rosi, my cherry-stone. On the day that heralded the beginning of the end, like all the other years, we were celebrating La Braukmann's birthday. This is the day.

BRAUKMANN. Colonel Wimp. All pigeons are high-fliers. All puffins are high-fliers. All pigs are high-fliers.

They all laugh.

SEIFFERT. Delish beestings. Ain't half delish.

LA BRAUKMANN. Made by yours truly.

BÜSCHER. What's in 'em?

LA BRAUKMANN. Well, what's in 'em is: a pint of rich creamy milk, a pinch of salt, sugar, currants, but only a few. And pastry.

SEIFFERT. Ain't half delish.

LA BRAUKMANN. So you eat without being forced to, Seiffert.

BÜSCHER. When it's beestings, he doesn't eat, he wolfs.

BRAUKMANN. Colonel Wimp. All wheatears are high-fliers. All queen ants are high-fliers. All anteaters are high-fliers.

They all laugh.

RUDI. By the way, Braukmann, we went on that holiday.

BRAUKMANN. Honestly?

RUDI. Didn't we, Rosi, my cherry-stone?

ROSI. Yes, it was heaven on earth.

RUDI. Where are the photos, Rosi, my cherry-stone, where are the photos?

ROSI. In the car.

RUDI. What are they in the car for, my cherry-stone, what are they in the car for?

ROSI. Should I ?

RUDI. Shift yourself, at the double.

BRAUKMANN. He is a one, our Rudi.

RUDI. My Rosi, my cherry-stone, she knows what I mean. You do know, don't you, Rosi?

ROSI (*about to go*). I do know.

RUDI. You see, she does know.

LA BRAUKMANN. What sort of holiday?

RUDI. An adventure holiday into the everlasting ice.

LA BRAUKMANN. Into the everlasting ice. Interesting.

RUDI. Yes, you can leave the whole lot behind you – work, day-to-day routine. You're in another world. We all need that every now and again. You get glued to your comfy chair. It dulls the senses. You get glued to your comfy chair.

ROSI. Here are the photos.

RUDI. My Rosi wheezes. She's forever puffing. She smokes like a smokestack. A real threat to the environment.

BRAUKMANN. He is a one, our Rudi.

RUDI. My Rosi, my cherry-stone, she knows what I mean. You do know, don't you Rosi?

ROSI. I couldn't get the door open at first. A quick turnover in motors.

RUDI. You see, she does know.

LA BRAUKMANN. Beestings, Seiffert.

SEIFFERT. Any time. Beestings, the Indians' favourite food.

BRAUKMANN. Help yourself, gents – and ladies – while rations last.

RUDI. This one's me on an ice-breaker.

BÜSCHER. Ice-breaker. Pity it's so small. And out of focus.

ROSI. Out of focus.

RUDI. Out of focus, my cherry-stone. But Rosi is in focus. This one's in focus, my Rosi in a bikini.

LA BRAUKMANN. In a bikini.

RUDI. Barbecuing on a glacier.

BÜSCHER. Barbecuing on a glacier, I could die laughing.

BRAUKMANN. Did they serve pemmican, too?

RUDI. Serve what?

BRAUKMANN. Pemmican.

LA BRAUKMANN. A knowledgeable man, Braukmann.

RUDI. Did they serve that, Rosi?

ROSI. Not so far as I know.

RUDI. But why didn't they serve it?

BRAUKMANN. Forget it, Rudi, forget it.

RUDI. This one's Rosi with a Ross seal.

LA BRAUKMANN. Rosi with a Ross seal.

ROSI. It was kind of sick-making.

RUDI. Now she tells me.

BÜSCHER. Rosi with a Ross seal. Just like the circus.

BRAUKMANN. Colonel Wimp. All eagles are high-fliers. All egrets are high-fliers. All Ross seals are high-fliers.

They all laugh.

RUDI. Together in the tent.

LA BRAUKMANN. Look, Braukmann, together in the tent, chance'd be a fine thing.

RUDI. You get one night in a tent.

BRAUKMANN. At that temperature.

RUDI. Bollocks. Oil-heaters, portable.

BÜSCHER. Everything laid on then, everything laid on.

RUDI. Doesn't come cheap, a holiday like that, doesn't come cheap.

LA BRAUKMANN. New supplies, Seiffert.

SEIFFERT. Ain't half delish. One for me.

BRAUKMANN. Beestings for an Indian.

RUDI. What's an Indian got to do with it?

SEIFFERT. I'm an Indian and I've got a good head for heights. Good head for heights Indian.

RUDI. This is the voice of Fate. Here's the scaffolding, there's good head for heights Indian.

SEIFFERT. Look for cheap dumboes in the Third World. Indians are as proud as Indians.

They all laugh.

LA BRAUKMANN. What else do you do, Rosi?

ROSI. Me?

LA BRAUKMANN. Yes, you.

RUDI. Smokes, smokes non-stop. Packets every day. She blows all my cash up the chimney.

BÜSCHER. That's over the top, Rudi.

RUDI. My Rosi, my cherry-stone, she knows what I mean. You do know, don't you, Rosi?

ROSI. Yes, yes, yes.

RUDI. You see, she does know.

A bell rings.

LA BRAUKMANN. Who's that?

BRAUKMANN. I'll go.

RUDI. Hang on. Probably a friend of the family to wish you many happy returns. The birthday girl must go herself.

BRAUKMANN. He's quite right there, our Rudi, where he's right, he's quite right.

LA BRAUKMANN. Well, just a sec.

SLUPIANEK (*in the doorway*). Greetings, Luise.

LA BRAUKMANN. Oh, a rose.

SLUPIANEK. A rose for a rose. But watch out, thorns.

BRAUKMANN. Say it with flowers. Come on in, Slupianek. Everyone's here. Even Rudi and Rosi.

SLUPIANEK. Sorry, in a hurry.

LA BRAUKMANN. Why are you in a hurry, then? You've got to have a cup of coffee. And I won't take no for an answer. You've got to have a cup of coffee.

SLUPIANEK. Just a coffee.

LA BRAUKMANN. You hurt, Slupianek?

SLUPIANEK. Not worth mentioning.

BRAUKMANN. How do, Slupianek.

SLUPIANEK. How do, Braukmann. How do, everyone.

LA BRAUKMANN. We're just looking at photos. Rudi and Rosi's. Adventure holiday into the everlasting ice.

BÜSCHER. A discerning palate.

LA BRAUKMANN. Slupianek, you're our expert, aren't you?

SLUPIANEK. The Sahara's more my line. Caravans, camels and sand.

BRAUKMANN. A chair for the Desert Fox.

SEIFFERT. Got any more beestings?

BRAUKMANN. The Indian as cake-cemetery. Big Chief Cake-Cemetery.

RUDI. On my left, Ricky Rabbit-punch. One time wrestler. Knows all the big names, Steve the Stretcher, the lot.

SLUPIANEK. Interesting group. And on your right?

RUDI. A Zürich business man. Eh, Rosi, my cherry-stone?

ROSI. Yes.

SLUPIANEK. Interesting group.

RUDI. Can't you ever stop smoking? It really is sick-making. This one's the Pole.

BRAUKMANN. The Pole.

RUDI. The Pole from the plane. That really is the Pole. You get a diploma, a certificate, handwritten, Doctor Soandso.

BÜSCHER. That really is the Pole.

RUDI. Really the Pole. Eh, Rosi, my cherry-stone?

ROSI. Yes.

RUDI. Terrif, no?

BÜSCHER. Landscape everywhere.

SEIFFERT. Were there dangerous crevasses?

RUDI. Yes, even crevasses.

BÜSCHER. Bit monotonous.

RUDI. That depends. This one.

BÜSCHER. Penguins.

LA BRAUKMANN. Penguins. Penguins.

BRAUKMANN. All penguins are high-fliers.

Silence.

SLUPIANEK. So that really is the Pole?

RUDI. No, a backyard in Herne.

ROSI. Very funny, my Rudi.

RUDI. Can't you ever stop smoking?

LA BRAUKMANN. I'll go and put the coffee on.

RUDI. Enjoying it, Seiffert?

SEIFFERT. The Big Chief gives you his thanks, Paleface.

RUDI. Firewater for the Big Chief.

BRAUKMANN. You're on, schnaps all round. Thanks, Rudi.

RUDI. What for, Braukmann?

BRAUKMANN. Well, schnaps and cigs.

RUDI. Bollocks, would I forget me old muckers? Eh, Rosi, my cherry-stone?

ROSI. No, no, no.

BRAUKMANN. Right then, cheers.

RUDI. To the birthday girl. Still without employment, Slupianek?

SLUPIANEK. No, just without work, Doctor.

RUDI. Aggressive, Slupianek, but I suppose it's understandable. Being out of work makes some people depressed and others aggressive. You don't look depressed. Look, the Indian is stuffing the delish beestings. Büscher, equally placid. And Braukmann, you old bugger –

LA BRAUKMANN. Braukmann's got a job.

RUDI. Is that right? Congratulations.

BRAUKMANN. Thanks.

RUDI. As I said, I suppose it's understandable. But jobs have got to be done. How did Hitler put it? Jobs give you freedom. Autobahns were his idea. Slick Dick, knew it all, had all the answers.

SLUPIANEK. Adolf, the man with all the answers.

RUDI. Stop it, Sonny, stop it. He was a man of ideas. Everyone knows what was wrong. But the autobahns. Who'd get an idea like that nowadays? No one. What d'we pay taxes for? For your betters to use their brains. Over poor sods like you, for instance, Slupianek. Not over monkeys in the jungle. So that you, you lot earn some money, that's the whole point. Then you'll be off the streets, not sitting around whinging, you'll stop sponging off the state, so that it could get up off its arse again. I die laughing, whenever I see it, straight up, I die laughing. OK, I'll shut up. Typical, when it comes to their own worries, no one ever listens. And Rosi keeps smoking. It really is sick-making. Take a look at La Braukmann, is she hooked on the weed? Begging your pardon, friends, I'll shut up.

SLUPIANEK. You're a world champion arsehole, Rudi.

RUDI. Like I said, aggressive.

ROSI (*opening her blouse*). I love the sun, the moon and the stars
But most of all I love you –

SEIFFERT. Annual fair in Dakota.

RUDI. At it again, eh? This smut of yours makes me throw up. Do up your front, you cunt.

Hits her.

SLUPIANEK. You're the cunt round here, Rudi, leathery and sweaty.

LA BRAUKMANN. You lot still haven't got beyond your bosom friend, with his Hitler, and the autobahns, the man with all the answers, you haven't shaved him yet. Come, Rosi, come.

ROSI (*going out with* LA BRAUKMANN). That warthog, I'll lay him out, that warthog.

RUDI. Come, Rosi, or I'll come for you.

SLUPIANEK. Büscher, let the dogs off the leash.

BÜSCHER. Including Lasse, my favourite.

SLUPIANEK. Including Lasse.

BÜSCHER (*pulls* FRANKIEBOY *out of his hiding-place.*). Lasse, heel.

RUDI. I'm going, wait till I get you home.

BÜSCHER. At 'im Lasse, at 'im.

They hurl themselves at RUDI.

Scene Twelve (b): At the Goal

SLUPIANEK. Was that something, Büscher?

BÜSCHER. That was something, Amundsen.

SLUPIANEK. What, Amundsen? Then I may say Hanssen.

BÜSCHER. Say it. Say Hanssen.

SEIFFERT. And Bjaaland.

BRAUKMANN. And Wisting.

BÜSCHER. Amundsen, let's do the last kilometrelets to the Pole.

SLUPIANEK. How many are there, Wisting?

BRAUKMANN. If it wasn't just a dream, 179.45.

SLUPIANEK. It isn't a dream.

BRAUKMANN. Right then, 179.45.

SLUPIANEK. One step to every Kmlet. How about it?

SEIFFERT. That makes 179 and nearly a half.

BRAUKMANN. Are we ready? Everyone present?

SLUPIANEK. Not everyone, Büscher. There were five, five. Come out of there, Luise. Here, Sverre Hassel, your gear.

BRAUKMANN. 179.45 to our goal.

LA BRAUKMANN. Lads, lads.

SLUPIANEK. Can a camel ride a bike?

BÜSCHER
SEIFFERT
BRAUKMANN } No, no, no.
LA BRAUKMANN

SLUPIANEK. Why not?

BÜSCHER
SEIFFERT
BRAUKMANN } Course not.
LA BRAUKMANN

SLUPIANEK. Because, because, because –

BÜSCHER
SEIFFERT
BRAUKMANN } He's got no thumb to ring the bell.
LA BRAUKMANN

SLUPIANEK. All present. All prepared.

BÜSCHER. Hang on. Frankieboy. Come on, my Lasse.

BRAUKMANN. I think Lasse passed over some time ago.

SEIFFERT. Straight ahead. Straight ahead with music.

EVERYONE. One, two, three . . . a hundred and seventy-eight, a hundred and seventy-nine . . . and nearly a half.

SLUPIANEK. The goal was reached and the journey finished.

SEIFFERT. And this cigar as a memento of the Pole.

LA BRAUKMANN. Pride and joy shone from the five pairs of eyes.

BRAUKMANN. Fists weak with frost grasped the flag and planted it there.

BÜSCHER. And even the weather was at its best.

Scene Thirteen: Endgame

The attic. On the washing line a Norwegian flag. SLUPIANEK *wearing furs and sitting in a chair; nearby, with a blanket,* FRANKIEBOY.

SLUPIANEK. What on earth's keeping Bjaaland? What's keeping Bjaaland? Wisting, do you know what's keeping Bjaaland?

BRAUKMANN (*coming in*). The Moose is at the jobcentre.

SLUPIANEK. Come again? Where is he?

BRAUKMANN. The jobcentre.

SLUPIANEK. I see.

BRAUKMANN. I'm for the high jump.

SLUPIANEK. Come again?

BRAUKMANN. No choice. Night shift. 'Bye.

SLUPIANEK. Braukmann.

BRAUKMANN. Yes.

SLUPIANEK. Do you remember how Bjaaland and his team fell into a giant crevasse in the ice at the devilish Hell's Gates?

BRAUKMANN. Yes.

SLUPIANEK. And how Hanssen shouted: Hang on, Bjaaland, stay where you are, I'll get the photographic apparatus. Do you remember?

BRAUKMANN. Yes.

SLUPIANEK. And how I, thinking the crevasse wasn't all that dangerous or full of snow, asked: What's it like, the crevasse? Do you remember?

BRAUKMANN. Yes.

SLUPIANEK. And what answer did Bjaaland give, as he was clinging to the sledge?

BRAUKMANN. Oh, just as you'd expect, bottomless.

SLUPIANEK. Was that something?

BRAUKMANN (*as he goes*). Yeah, that was something.

SLUPIANEK. You can get used to anything. Even the greatest danger.

BÜSCHER (*coming in*). By the way, Benno, I'm leaving, for good. Canada.

SLUPIANEK. Aha. Watch out, Büscher, crevasses, really dangerous crevasses.

BÜSCHER (*as he goes*). Yeah.

SLUPIANEK. I see. Canada.

LA BRAUKMANN (*off*). Yeah yeah, tomorrow. But not the red geraniums, not the red ones.

SLUPIANEK. Totally wrong-headed and disastrous.

LA BRAUKMANN (*coming in with food*). Hello there, Benno. At the stall, there was
pandemonium again today. Two hundredweight of chips I had to do. Two hundredweight.
People go on guzzling. They all moan, but go on guzzling. Two hundredweight of chips and
a bucket of salad cream. A bucket. Right after dinner in the canteen, they make a beeline for
me. I'm their afters. They witter on till my ears explode, smacking their lips. They
complain about God and the world, with chips between their teeth. Moaning and stuffing,
complaining and guzzling, griping and gulping. Rubbing grease into their fingers. They're
chockful of misery and choking as they guzzle.

SLUPIANEK. And you, Luise?

LA BRAUKMANN. The smoke from the stall gets in my eyes, gets in my lungs and even gets
in my heart.

SLUPIANEK. What about the lemon?

LA BRAUKMANN (*as she goes*). Even a lemon doesn't help. For Christ's sake, Slupianek.

SLUPIANEK. What on earth's keeping Bjaaland?
Seiffert is at the jobcentre again. He set off pretty early. He's still bleary-eyed but wide
awake and raring to go. The white-washed vestibule. A notice board, rooms, floors, right,
left, straight ahead. Go straight ahead. Hold the course. Do I wander off to the right? No. To
the left? Don't wander off to the left, you're obsessed by the left, raving leftie. Straight
ahead, for ever straight ahead. A block of ice. No, a staircase. To the first floor. Step by step.
Watch out, crevasses in the ice. Is there a bridge of snow anywhere? The last step, the first
floor. A glass door. A long, grey-black polished corridor. Fluorescent lights on the ceiling.
Long wooden benches crammed full of penguins. Nothing but penguins sitting there,
keeping quiet, their heads bowed. No space to sit down. Standing room only. Ahead, the
door that meant hope. It's white, white. What's behind it? The South Pole. Is that where the
Pole actually is? Really and truly, or only from the plane? Perhaps it's only a wall of ice.
Sheer, unclimbable. What am I saying, unclimbable? What are my ice-pick and crampons
for? Hacking out steps. Click click. Step by step. Breath comes in spasms. Freezes
immediately on your fur and goggles. I can't see a thing any more. But still, on, on. Remove
that curtain. It isn't your turn yet, yells a penguin. Paws off that curtain. A penguin leaves.
A bit of a bench becomes free. On no account sit down, on no account. If you're sitting
down you fall asleep and freeze to death, easy as pie. When's my turn? Be patient, it takes
time, please be patient. A pink cloud. I fall asleep, God help me, I fall asleep standing up.
How much time has passed? The door is open. Come in. Filing cabinets right and left. Don't
lose your way. Straight ahead. Hold the course. Do sit down. No, I won't sit down, says
Seiffert. Do you want me to freeze to death? We've got oil-heaters, portable. Would you
like a coffee? Yes, coffee, says Seiffert, a gulp of hot coffee. To wash down the lump in my
throat. And you are? Bjaaland, says Seiffert. Funny name. We haven't got that in our files.
Well then, says Seiffert, Adams. Yes, Adams, says Seiffert, I'm called Adams. Why are you
gaping? I, says Seiffert, and you must excuse me, am snowblind. I, says Seiffert, am a
moose and snowblind. A snowblind moose. Ponies, says Seiffert, are in any case better than
dogs. They have to be shot. Rosi, says Seiffert, got a slip made of seal-skin. I beg you, says
Seiffert, on bended knees, for a job on an ice-breaker. On an ice-breaker? No, says Seiffert,
with a nice baker. I demand, yells Seiffert, a job with a nice baker. Yes, I am perfectly calm,
says Seiffert. Yes, says Seiffert, I will sit down. You've got to telephone, says Seiffert, I
understand. Yes, says Seiffert, I understand. Yes, says Seiffert, I quite understand. Any
minute now two nice men will appear, because I'm far too cold in this thin jacket, in all this
ice and snow. Yes, says Seiffert, they are good friends. They, says Seiffert, have my best
interests at heart. Yes, they have a lovely warm jacket for me. But I don't want it, yells
Seiffert. What are windows for?

SLUPIANEK. What on earth's keeping Bjaaland? The blanket.

FRANKIEBOY. Let me keep it, Amundsen, otherwise I'll get so cold. We are at the South Pole, after all.

SLUPIANEK. So, we are at the South Pole.

FRANKIEBOY. Course.

SLUPIANEK. And where is the South Pole?

FRANKIEBOY. Somewhere south of Herne.

A child cries. SLUPIANEK *takes off his furs, goes out.*

MAN TO MAN

Man to Man was first performed at the Traverse Theatre, Edinburgh, on 30 July 1987, and transferred to the Royal Court Theatre, London on 4 January 1988 with Tilda Swinton in the role of MAX GERICKE.

Directed by Stephen Unwin
Designed by Bunnie Christie
Lighting by Beb Ormrod

MAX GERICKE:

One

WHEN THE RED SUN SINKS IN THE WATERS NEAR CAPRI
Those holiday cruises back in Hitler's time
Were really something. You could eat butter
By the spoonful. And much much more.
On trips called STRENGTH THROUGH JOY
A working man could sail to Norway's fjords – and get back –
For seven marks a day. Germany was vast.
It stretched from Western France to Eastern Poland.
Now it doesn't even get as far as Brandenburg.
My pension keeps me going – that and beer.
There's lots of scroungers on the streets these days.
They say they're unemployed. I say they're workshy.
Where there's a will . . . As Hitler said: ARBEIT MACHT FREI.
I earn some pocket-money on the side
By dressing up as a Turkish char. You do what you can.

Two

THERE SHE STOOD ROOTED TO THE SPOT TOO FRIGHTENED AND TOO
HORRIFIED TO MOVE BUT THEY HAD ALREADY HEATED UP THE IRON
SLIPPERS OVER A COAL FIRE AND WHEN THEY HAD BROUGHT THEM IN WITH
TONGS AND PUT THEM DOWN ON THE FLOOR BESIDE HER SHE HAD TO STEP
INTO THE RED-HOT SHOES AND DANCE UNTIL SHE DROPPED DOWN DEAD

There was one thing my Ma could do better than anyone else – morning, noon and night, she'd just sit there quietly making brown paper bags, 10,000 a day, and in return for this staggering feat she was paid the princely sum of two marks, that's twenty pfennigs a thousand.

Three

The doctor who shouts: I CAN'T GIVE YOU ANY TREATMENT FOR THAT when he sees the blister on my heel: SERVES YOU RIGHT FOR RUNNING BAREFOOT THROUGH WET GRASS.

The cobbler who laughs when he sees the thin piece of leather my Ma's brought, expecting he could make a new sole for my worn-out old shoe with it.

The scripture master who's so worried about scabies he rubs alcohol into his pupils' hands every morning.

Phrases like: FUCKING BONKERS or WHAT A FUCKING FUCK-UP or THERE'S SPUNK ALL OVER MY HAND.

Sentences like: I CAN SLAVE TILL I DROP FOR ALL YOU CARE or STRAIGHTEN THAT TABLECLOTH OR THE BOGEYMAN WILL GET YOU or THESE THINGS HAPPEN IN THE BEST OF FAMILIES.

The word HELVETIA on a postage stamp. Saying it out loud, really slowly, making a meal of it: HELVETIA.

The farmer's son who'll hand his sister over to the other lads if they'll do his work for him, while he sits by the pond and plays with his penknife.

Four

Looking for work is fucking hard work.
A schnaps. A beer. Both feet in the bowl.
Your arse gets bigger and bigger all the time
From all that sitting in all those corridors.
The same old questions and the same old lies.
SHE WAS ALL ALONE IN ALL THAT ICE AND SNOW.

Five

My first man was a volunteer from Saxony
A chronic drunk and brilliant with it.
He ran from hole to hole and over bodies dead and dying
And used me as a transit camp *en route*.
My second fella was my big romance.
We loved each other madly, as they say.
But he got drowned before the wedding.
I really was unlucky with my men.

By nineteen I was married. My Dad said: Well, you can wave goodbye to youth and innocence, and all that's special and unique. My marriage lasted one year, seven months, and twelve days. My husband was a crane-operator with Nagel and Sons. He wasn't a bad sort, and he did have a job. I'd heard about that before I'd heard his name. I did find out his name later though, but what I didn't know was that the sciatica, which'd been bothering him for years, was cancer. We got to know each other in a country restaurant. He drank beer. I drank *Weisse mit Schuss*. He took me back to his room. His chair was his wardrobe, so I had to sit on the bed. He kneeled at my feet and unbuttoned my blouse. So this is what paradise is like, I thought to myself, and said: I love you. You don't have to overdo it, he said, but I said it again: I love you. And when we'd slept together he said: No tits, your arse too tight, you look to me like fucking Snow White. I had to laugh. And then he tried to write Snow White on my wet belly. His finger was all yellow from too much smoking. Even now, whenever I hear anyone say Snow White I come over all peculiar. But we wasn't to be happy for long. So as not to lose his job, Max kept on going to work day after day, illness or no illness, but hardly ever bothered to see the doctor. The sodding sciatica was making his life hell.

His hand, now boneless, manages once again
To operate the gear-stick and controls,
To unwrap his bread and dripping, lift a cup,
Pull his cap right down over his face
To hide his yellow cheeks, and open up
His shirt, to give that sweat-soaked body
A breath of air; but Daddy Cancer
Sends his daughters on the rampage,
And feeds them Max's last remaining bones, and joints, and veins.
So now from sleep to sleep
From one day's work to another
With only his braces holding him together
He drags the half-eaten shell his body has become.
A ray of hope lights up the gloom:

His hand can raise a glass and stroke
His wife's behind, but soon
His hands go, his legs, and then his head and belly.
His body starts to shrivel up. Snow White
Acquires a dwarf.

At work, the guy Max had most contact with was called Erwin – his trousers always had a razor-sharp crease and his nickname was The Best Dressed Man in Mecklenburg. So, when I'd made up mind that come what may I'd take over my husband's job as a crane-operator at Nagel and Sons, it was Erwin I was most afraid would recognise me. So I cut off my hair and altered my husband's clothes and then, to help me through the first few days, I pretended I'd fallen downstairs. I hoped that by winding bandages round my head, by wearing a sort of disguise, if you like, my work-mates would gradually get used to the new face of Max Gericke. It was risky but I had no choice. I think I must've started planning it before my husband died, because, without knowing why, and much to his amazement, I had got him to explain how everything in the control cabin worked, and describe it down to the last detail. Against all expectation, I was able to carry out my plan quite easily, mainly because while he was working away up there in the control cabin my late lamented husband hardly ever spoke to any of his mates. Except for The Best Dressed Man in Mecklenburg, who used to scurry up the ladder every now and again to get away from a sticky situation down below. Beggars can't be choosers, and apart from the odd minor cock-up manoeuvring crates around, which the others put down to my accident, I did bloody well. Unfortunately, as a result of these extraordinary events, my dear departed ended up getting a cut-price funeral in some provincial town, with his widow's name carved on the gravestone. Here lies Ella Gericke, born in Frankfurt-an-der-Oder, died of cancer. R.I.P. Jesus Christ, the nerve of the woman.

And on the third day he rose again from the dead.
I had to rise the next day at five a.m.
I, my own widow, my late lamented husband, had to be
Man enough to wear the fucking trousers.
Why was being a woman not enough?

Six

The church I could avoid, but not the boozer.
Can't you play scat? No. Fucking arsehole.
You come with us tonight. We'll soon show you how.
A table. A French deck of cards. A beer.
That was the beginning and possibly the end.
You can't score. Show your hand. A ten on its own.
One guy's already shuffled off his mortal coil.
A spade. Call it a spade. A club. I've joined it.
Put your cards on the table. Max. A queen.
Faint hearts ne'er won fair lady. Diamonds are a girl's best friend. My head is spinning.
And beer and schnaps all churned up together
And schnaps and beer and fill them up again.
A man's gut don't easily call it a day.
BEER WOMAN HERE WOMAN BEER BEER BEER
And with the next round they order pickled leg of pork,
With onions, peas and mustard on the side.
No pork? What's up? Not kosher?
Bet you're circumcised. Bet you're not called Max
Gericke at all, but Nathan Rosenberg.
And two fine specimens of German manhood rise,
Tottering, to their feet. Eat or die.

Inside me schnaps and beer are fighting beer and schnaps.
Eat or die. It's good enough for us.
I'm seeing pinky-red flags flying over the North Pole.
Then I see nothing, then I see it all –
There stands my Ma with her book of fairy-tales,
A mountain of porridge. Porridge turns to pork.
Eat or die. Your last chance.
I chew, I swallow, it won't go down.
Eat or die. Show us what you've got.
I go on eating. Or is it eating me?
Am I the pig? Is pork the thing to be?
Eat or die. Now, only bones are left.
So beautifully bare. Picked so clean.
So white. So naked. So wonderfully stripped.
I wave the bones in triumph once I've done –
Then bawl out: ICH BIN EIN DEUTSCHER MANN!

Seven

I melt the frost flowers at the kitchen window with my breath.
Out in the yard a violent battle starts.
The battle-lines confront each other grimly,
Their weapons ready in their freezing hands.

They piss a hammer and sickle in the snow.
And, not to be outdone, the next-door kids
Squeeze out their last remaining drops
To draw a line of swastikas in the snow.

Eight

Looking at my belly, I felt sick
Desperately longing to have a child.
A pillow down your trousers – hey, presto! – pregnant.
It hurts. It punches. It bounces. And it tugs.
MY PEACE IS GONE MY HEART IS SORE
Ach, this fullness feels so wonderful, so terrifying
IT'S GONE FOR EVER YES EVERMORE
It's choking me. I'm being torn apart. I'm bursting.
It must come out. It doesn't want to, but it must.
Ach, this emptiness, wonderful yet terrifying.
A beer. A beer. And sod the rest.
It cries. It's alive. It's got ten fingers,
Two eyes, a nose and a cock.
Come here, to my bosom, boy, and drink.
Now you're getting bigger and bigger. First words:
Car and ball. First steps.
Where are you going? Straight for the boozer?
You want to be a sailor – an explorer, a boxer?
Make something of your life, my lad.
Too late for me. Too soon for you.
Come here, pillow – here, between my thighs,
You're more use there than in my belly.

Nine

Then came the time of battles and of riots.
The jungle was a safer place than Prussia.
You can get used to anything in time
– As my old Dad would say – even good news.
As many meetings as grains of sand on the shore.
The stink of sweat, the air
So solid you could cut it into cubes.
No sooner has the magic word been uttered: SOCIALISM
The doors fly open. Shouts, clubs.
The crowd first sways to one side, then
The other. Tables, mirrors, windows, chairs
Are used as weapons and missiles.
Oppressors and oppressed hit out at, kick,
And fasten claws and teeth on one another.
Where is the end and where is the beginning?
It's like a snake that's swallowed its own tail
Some idiot grabs me in the groin –
He yanks, he squeezes, pulls and can't believe
His groping hand has no effect.

The chairs all legless. All the windows smashed.
Table-legs are clubs. Bits of glass are knives.
Blood washes the smoke-stained walls.
And women jump out the windows, screaming –
Me included. Thirty women and one man.
I wasn't pro-Rotfront, nor Siegheil neither
More like somewhere in between – pro-Number One:
My job, my own concerns.
A beer. A schnaps. And bugger all the rest.
But one fine day it dawns on me:
A vote for Hitler is a vote for war. And war's
Bad news for me. Armies need soldiers.
That night I have a terrifying dream:
A big long table with a doctor and some other men –
Yours truly at his medical.
A dozen pairs of eyes are staring at me.
I feel as if they want to rip
Away my face and peer inside.
The doctor tilts his head, looks down.
Keeps staring at my fly, and then
With a disgusting, half-bent finger fumbles
With my clothing. He undoes button after button,
Slowly pulling my shirt-tail out.
The finger creeps down inside my trousers.
He fiddles about, and then – still in my dream –
Suddenly pulls out a rabbit.
One foot is missing. The stump is bloody. Then
– Still in my dream – the animal gets bigger and bigger
And keeps on growing, like an elephant,
And still it keeps getting bigger – like a tree, a hill, the sea.
Then – still in my dream – pitch blackness everywhere.
A womb, which I'm inside. A terrifying silence
Rumbling in my ears. I wake up:
The nightmare's just beginning: Hitler's got in.

Ten

I dread that time between the wolf's howl and the barking of a dog:
Between the darkest night and faintest glimmering of dawn –
Too tired to sleep, too drowsy to wake up, incapable of dream and thought.
Your weary body helpless. Your head like lead.
My last remaining hope is under my mattress –
A small, rectangular piece of card
Carefully hidden from all strangers' eyes.
My passport, or, to be exact, my widow's.
If I am called up, if I'm summoned to a medical
The plan is: I'll slip back into *her* skin,
Take off my suit, unknot my tie,
And take refuge in a blouse and skirt.
But what's to become of him, the man I am?
And me? The woman I want to be?
I think myself back and I think myself forward.
Who? Where, when, how come I got like this?
Where from? Going where? Your head is spinning.
Frau Müller from next door's already up.
With seven mouths all crying out for food
What massive cooking-pots she must have. The clock
Strikes five. It's time to wear the trousers.

Eleven

Still needed here to keep the home fires burning
But for how much longer can I avoid the Front?
We men are getting scarcer all the time –
Nagel and Sons are taking women now.
The scroungers on the streets are ordered to report
For duty in the forests – building autobahns
For the Reich, while many others vanish
Never to be seen again, and with them goes
The Best Dressed Man in Mecklenburg.
As they lead him from the site I hear them say:
Thank God your badge is pink, sweetheart, not red –
You queers are only sent to concentration camps.

Twelve

Puppchen, they all called her – the new canteen lady, I mean. PUPPCHEN, DU BIST MEIN PUPPCHEN. The lads would've gladly queued up and spent their last pfennig on her. And there's no two ways about it – she was a stunner. But what puzzled me was this: why did she always give me a much bigger portion than anybody else? Why did I always get offered a second helping of stewed fruit? After work why did she hang about at the site-gate waiting for me to walk her home? And when we got to her front door, why did she always kiss me goodnight? In that case, you must be the Prince, was all she said when I told her I already had a girl: Snow White, white as snow, red as blood, black as ebony. But I wasn't the Prince. In fact I wasn't even the crane-operator Max Gericke. Or was I? Or what? Suddenly I felt the same pain I'd felt years ago, when they fished my fiancé out the Havel, white as snow. And even earlier, many many years before, when the baker's son, who I worshipped, left our home town to go to another school somewhere else. That was the first time – when I realised I'd never see him again – that I felt this incredible emptiness inside: this pain deep in my belly. Not like they tell you – in your heart, but much further down, right in your guts. And here it was again. I broke away from her and ran all the way home. On the pavement outside my house some kids were playing THE THIN BLACK LINES OF DEATH AND THE BIG SOFT SLABS OF GOD. I climb the stairs. More kids. We've got two dogs, says one: a poodle and a knife-grinder. What kind of animal is that? Knife-grinder? Never heard of it! But lots of animals are called knife-grinder. Away, I open the door, and go into the kitchen, forgetting to close the front door. Then I sit down in my chair and just stare at the wall. PUPPCHEN, DU BIST MEIN PUPPCHEN. God, it's great to be one of your chosen ones – but I'm a knife-grinder. In walks THE THIN BLACK LINE OF DEATH. The door was open, Herr Gericke. Is anything wrong? You look a bit . . . No, nothing's wrong. I'm a knife-grinder. THE THIN BLACK LINE OF DEATH shuts the door behind him. Everything's fine! I shout after him. My God, this pain in my guts. And I am a knife-grinder. Why am I a knife-grinder?

Thirteen

Barking with fury in his husky voice
Block-custodian Wollonzen runs from door to door.
He's distinctly heard the Bumbumbum Bum
Of the illegal BBC transmitter.
A tip-off indicates the upper storey.
I'm in the clear, I haven't got no radio. Still,
The block-custodian searches everywhere,
Opens the wardrobe and then taps on the walls.
And suddenly there it is: Bumbumbum Bum –
Thus the traitor, by himself betrayed,
Is discovered on the balcony drumming out
His treasonable signals on the wall
Of his hutch. It's Egon the rabbit.
First a source of extra meat,
Then an extra mouth to feed,
Now a source of treasonable transmissions.
The block-custodian is beside himself, and all
The neighbours are crying out for blood.
No matter how I cried, it didn't help –
They lined him up against his hutch – and shot him.

Fourteen

Night falls. There's a knock on my door.
I love you, and I've come to tell you, Max.
Come in then, *Puppchen*, take a seat, relax.
My darling Max, I'm dead unless you help me.
Oh, come on, *Puppchen*, Germany
Is full of men. My Snow White is the girl who fits
My bill – I love her big round bum and bouncing tits.
And now my *Puppchen* ought to go to bed.
But Max, I don't know where to lay my head.
It isn't easy to explain –
Tonight a lot of people will be slain.
I've got involved in politics, you see –
And now I can't – I won't – break free.

It's hard to know how much to say
I've been on the run since yesterday.
They're after me, you see I'm a red,
And if they find me, soon I will be dead.
I said: Under my mattress hidden from view
I've something I want to give to you –
A dead woman's passport – there's nothing more to say
We kissed, and Ella Gericke went on her way.

Fifteen

This was the cell. Grey walls. A cement floor. A concrete coffin, in fact. A plank hinged to the wall. In the up position. At night this plank became a bed. Ninety centimetres wide, one metre seventy long, fixed on the slant, and without any raised area for the head. This plank was all you had to sleep on – no blanket, no mattress, no pillow. For that you used your shoes. When the plank is up, where do you sit? There isn't even a stool. The plank stays up all day long. So you've got to stay standing. Dawn to dusk. On your feet the whole day. All you can do is take four steps forward and four steps back. From five in the morning till nine at night. The whole day. And if the SA man doesn't fold the plank down, the whole night as well. Sitting on the floor is forbidden. As the SA man says: Any prisoner found sitting on the floor will be severely punished. So you've no choice but to stay on your feet from dawn to dusk. But if you stand for too long you get water on the knee. So the only thing you can do is keep walking: walk, walk, walk, forward, then back, four steps to the window, four steps to the door, to the window, to the door, to the window, to the door, window, door. At five o'clock every morning, the SA man bawls out: Plank up! And then the same endless day starts all over again, and goes on till about nine, when the SA man comes in again and

A schnaps. A schnaps. You've heard it all now
SA man Gericke was a Frau.
Snow White and the Seven Dwarves.
How else could I avoid the medical?

Sixteen

Then came May, nineteen forty-five.
WHO IN THIS APPALLING CARNAGE
Can contain these Russians? Who
WILL PROTECT US FROM THIS WORLD OF ENEMIES
Our last reserves of children and old men
Stood manfully at the ready in the woods of Brandenburg.
But I – like a pig in shit – stayed put,
Fighting on my favourite Front: a castle in the Marches,
Guarding supplies with three other gentlemen
Who were destined never to reach the Front.
Crammed to the brim with uniforms,
With hypodermics, bandages and crutches,
Tents and shovels – all created
TO BURY THE FALLEN OF BOTH ARMIES
For me the sheer size of the castle was a blessing –
A room to myself gave me protection. All the same
I trained myself to sleep face down.
When I looked out my window I could see
No corpses, no tanks, no craters –

What I saw was stags, just browsing by a pond
On which some bright coloured drakes were swimming,
Their grey ducks trailing after.
AM I AWAKE OR DREAMING AM I ALIVE AND CONSCIOUS
Here, no murderous hail of bullets flies
Towards me. Here, among these hills and bushes.
We, a little band of German brothers,
Are still protected from this world of enemies.
LIKE A VAST TIDE OF SLAUGHTER BULLETS
GRENADES AND GRAPESHOT SWEPT TOWARDS US
As for my mates, they sunned themselves
By the pond, fringed with weeping willows.
They showed each other their cocks and jerked off.
I can't swim, I can't stand the sun, I just watched.
What's up? Can't find your cock?
Come on, show us. Trousers down. You fucking coward.
I buggered off. They followed me. I fell.
Ran on. Stumbled. I had to make the village.
They hid their pricks with their hands.
Then retreated, laughing: you'll be back!
STAY STANDING AT YOUR POST TILL FURTHER ORDERS
There was I, leaning against a tree. My God,
I had none to stand at, and the whole of Poland wide open.
What's to be done, cries Zeus, the gods are drunk.

In the Neustadtmarkt cabaret show
A dancer called Fred
Who's lanky and slow
Delights and regales
The admiring females
With the paw of a hare
He's put you-know-where.

I saw myself as a hunter stalking deer.
And if a man who's drowning clutches at a straw
The one I was stuck with was a bent hare's paw.
But soon the Russians made my problems vanish:
Artillery salvoes pulverised
My naked comrades in the sands of Brandenburg.

Seventeen

As Russian tanks got nearer, off I ran
Westwards – to reach the Elbe was my plan.
But suddenly my way is barred
By two SS men standing guard.
Halt, deserter, where are you trying to go?
I'm only wearing this uniform for show.
Goebbels drove me to it, in fact:
Dressed as a woman, I might be attacked.
The Russians rape you first, then chop
Your breasts off – that's what I want to stop.
Come on then, Komrad, show us your tits
And arse – let's teach you how a German rider sits
In your saddle – this is how it's done –

So once in that war I got to use my gun.

It never rains but it pours. When I was seven, my Dad gave up his job in a provincial town and moved to Berlin to work for Borsig. The idea was we'd join him once he'd found somewhere to live and'd got settled in. When he came to visit us one day, riding in the mail-van, which was very expensive, he was so shocked by the way my Ma looked, he sent for the doctor. That was very expensive too. When the doctor had finished, he took my Dad to one side and told him he'd leave a prescription and call back in a day or two to see if anything could be done. But it was too late, and in no time at all my Ma had died of galloping consumption. It was a hard winter, and outside the ground was icy. My Dad fell over and sprained his right hand. And so, as a kid of seven, I was lumbered with all the housework. But first, I had to wash my Ma's body and put the lace nightcap on her head. Everybody who came to the house sang my praises and told me what a good girl I was, and nobody knew how terrified I was by the fact of death.

Eighteen

In the Emsland they don't need girls but lads.
There's too few men to work the land.
You've been one for so long, why not a few weeks longer?
Why not stay a man in this Sodom and Gomorrah
And – to be on the safe side – get
Another poor little rabbit's foot.

The citizens took all their goods to the peasants:
Their sheets and their pillows and their carpets,
To swap them for a pound of butter, or a few potatoes.
And schnaps exchanged for coupons
Bought a meal. Nowadays of course
You can wet your whistle with it every day.

As a farmlad I get the hardest work to do.
Your day begins at four. The cattle
Eat and shit, and then for a change, they shit and eat.
Then you do battle in the fields with hay and beet.
You flush out potatoes. Ambush cabbages. Machine-gun carrots.
My first response to being underfed –
Turnips and boiled swede for breakfast
And for tea boiled swede and turnips –
My first response is to get much stronger
Than I've ever been – and develop the muscles of a Hercules.
But the daily slog gnaws me to the bone.
I see the farmgirl feeding the chickens,
Milking cows. That's hard work too, I think, but still.
I skive off when I can. Which isn't often.
Sometimes I black out, but know
My days here are numbered. And then the farmer
Leads the talk around to women. Tells me the farmgirl
Is good for working but nothing else.
She's too stuck up to let him stick it up her.
Between ourselves, I tell him, I know a randy cunt,
Who's able and willing, and knows a thing or two.
She'll do anything for a sackful of grain.
Night comes. So does the farmer, emptying his sack
But filling mine with chicken-feed –

Not, as he'd promised, first-class wheat.
But even that sack of chicken-feed
Helped get me through the darkest days.
Ground in the coffee-mill first thing
It made a bowl of soup to last all day.
And now I'm slurping it again in my old flat –
Safe from bombs but not from thieves.
Now that the Emsland's in the West
The farmers get cheap labour from the East:
They come in their droves and gladly.

Nineteen

THINK HOW YOU'D ENJOY IT IF YOU'D FOUND
A LONG WHITE CIGARETTE TO SMOKE
NO NEED TO PICK UP ODD BUTTS FROM THE GROUND
OH JOHNNY GI LET ME SHARE YOUR FAG
PLEASE JOHNNY GI GIVE ME A DRAG

Sometimes, if I close my eyes, I see
In a village somewhere in the Marches
Of Brandenburg, now in the Russian Zone,
A cemetery before me. And by a grave
A prince. He kneels and kisses the earth
Which opens wide – Snow White climbs out,
Shaking earth off and unravelling the roots
Entwined around her. Tenderly
The Prince caresses her and she becomes
As white as snow, as red as blood,
As black as ebony. Away he carries her
To his mod. con. flat
With fridge and running hot and cold. Then off they go
To the Caucasus for their honeymoon.
And so Max Gericke can rest in peace
In that chilly earth, knowing Snow White, alias Ella,
Is now in the Red East, her conscience never blackened.

Twenty

For three whole years I nail together vegetable-crates
At Paule Packaging. One hundred crates a day.
But then, when Paul goes bust, a man from Hanover
Buys up the lot and starts demolishing
The workshop and the storeroom:
You won't get on unless you can be drastic!
This Karl-Friedrich Kaste undertakes to take me on –
I start producing plastic and elastic.
I pull a little handle at the front, and out
From the back a thousand plastic punnets pop.
You'll be stuck here for ever and a day, I tell myself.
Here stand you, and you can do no other.
In front of you, the handle, and behind, the punnets.
Do I turn the handle, or does it turn me?

Am I the handle – is the handle me?
At night I dream I'm God Almighty
Making whole universes out of plastic,
And over everything Kaste stands majestic
Cashing in on plastic and elastic.
But even God creates for six days only
And on the seventh takes a breather,
And thinks of something much less energetic.
There is all that plastic and elastic,
And there is Herr Karl-Friedrich Kaste – static.
So God knocks back a big swig from his bottle
And, half-pissed, comes up with an antidote:
Next Saturday, Karl-Friedrich Kaste, who's myopic,
Sees this attractive woman in his local.
She catches his eye because he catches hers.
He sends her a glass of sekt and thinks: fantastic!
But before Karl-Friedrich gets romantic
I've spent three weeks – which nearly drives me frantic –
Turning out his plastic and elastic.

And Saturday Night comes round again
MORE PEOPLE DIE OF BEER THAN DID OF BOMBS
And Kaste meets the woman in his local.
Over sekt and salmon, schnaps and sauerbraten
They get acquainted. Kaste's horny for her
And lures the little lady to his love-nest.
They say four eyes see more than two,
I'm the one with four – Kaste's blind –
OH LOVE DIVINE IS HEAVEN'S SWEETEST GIFT
With heavenly guidance, Kaste changes tactic
Because he knows that plastic and elastic,
If made by gentle women's hands – for much less pay –
Come cheaper. And by the time we get to May
Karl-Friedrich's been miraculously economic.
So now the work that used to drive me frantic
Producing piles of plastic and elastic
Has all been whisked away.
Prost!

THE SUN IS OUT THE SKY IS BLUE
DEAR LADY LET ME WALK WITH YOU

The factory would gladly take on Turks
But no more workers was allowed to immigrate.
So Heaven sends Kaste inspiration –
He smuggles Turkish blokes in by disguising them
As women here to visit their beloved husbands.
So far, so good. But the competition soon
Gets wind of it. The gaff is blown. The game is up.
The whole caboodle's up in smoke.
Karl-Friedrich Kaste's now cast as the villain.
And at his trial he wants the little lady as a witness.
But so far Heaven hasn't sent a sign.

Twenty-one

The Bible tells of seven fat years
Consumed by seven that was lean.
I eat my iron rations up
In seven weeks. HALLELUYA.

Twenty-two

Max Gericke is on the streets again,
Though now they're full of cars and made of asphalt.
Five years to go until I get his pension.
Hope springs eternal: Nagel and Sons
Require crane-operator, 2,000 marks a month.
He reads the ad. Tips up.
They're bound to know your face, he tells himself –
But Nagel and his Sons are Uncle Sam's.

Twenty-three

There's life in the old dog yet
Even old iron can lose its rust.
Go on, roast your face under a sun-ray lamp
And work your chest-expander a hundred and fifty times

DON'T WORRY LIFE BEGINS AT SIXTY-SIX
There's loads of vitamins in parsley
YOU'RE NEVER TOO OLD TO LEARN NEW TRICKS
So don't become a wallflower at the party.

Oh sure. Dead right. Not half. I'll say. Fuck Christmas!
All it does is cost you money
And make you cry your little eyes out.

A few years back I heard about a Commie
Who did away with Christmas altogether –
On Christmas Eve he read Karl Marx out loud.
Yet that same night slunk into a wood
And cut a tree down with his axe.

Twenty-four

Put your feet up, have a beer.
You've earned a break, Max, the hard life ends here.
There's telly to be watched – no need to pay.
You start at ten and go on goggling all day.
Theft, fraud and murder – once in a while –
All pensioners enjoy a juicy trial.

Defendant, is your name Leukoff?
Yes, my name is Leukoff, I'm from Bremen, East Frisland.
But it says here your name is Calmot, nationality French.

No, my name is Leukoff.
Our records show you're also known as Leupoff, Lenthoff and Leukowskie.

No, my name is Leukoff.
Your accent isn't East Frisian. More
Like French than anything.
I can't speak a word of French.
Well then, are you mentally disturbed?
No, I'm not mentally disturbed.

You were caught shoplifting. We're not going to chop your head off for it. But tell us who you
are.
My name's Leukoff.

Twenty-five

If you haven't got a job, make one.
Scatter a box of matches, pick them up.
FOR MOST OF HIS LIFE A SOLDIER STANDS
YOU BLINK AND GET A FIST BETWEEN YOUR EYES
WITH LOADED GUN AND IDLE HANDS
NAPOLEON WAS A WOMAN IN DISGUISE
OFFICIAL SOURCES IN THE DDR BELIEVE
THE YANKS ARE BOMBING THEM WITH COLORADO BEETLES
A PAINTER WITH ONLY ONE EAR
NAPOLEON ADAM OR EVE
MAX GERICKE BURIED IN FOREIGN EARTH
SPECIAL PICKLED PORK FOR ALL OF US
WHAT YOU'VE GOT IS WHAT YOU'RE WORTH
A DACHA SOMEWHERE IN THE CAUCASUS
THE WAR IS OVER NOW BUT AT A COST
WHETHER IT'S ZARAH LEANDER OR THE FUCKING FÜHRER
COLUMBUS PICKS UP THE BALL THAT HIMMLER LOST
EMPTY BOTTLES GIVE THE GAME AWAY
AND EARS HAVE WALLS SO CAREFUL WHAT YOU SAY
WHETHER IT'S ZARAH LEANDER OR THE FUCKING FUEHRER
ANOTHER NIGHT OF RUBBISH ON THE TELLY.

Twenty-six

The mirror makes me puke: death creeping up in slippers.
Mirror, mirror on the wall
Who is the fairest of them all?

Max Gericke, you are the fairest in this place
But over the hills and far away
Where the Seven Dwarves toil all day
Snow White is a thousand times fairer of face.

Appendix: Source material for CONQUEST OF THE SOUTH POLE and
MAN TO MAN

MAN TO MAN
A Short History of *Jacke Wie Hose*

Some time or other
Somewhere or other someone or other told me the story of a young woman who attempted, during the Great Depression, to hold on to the job her late husband had had. To do this, she stepped into the role of the deceased through disguise and other forms of artifice. Apparently, however, the attempt soon came to grief. A newspaper article revealed all.

Some time later
Whilst reading Brecht's short story: **Der Arbeitsplatz** I discover that, he Brecht, also knew about this episode.

Early 1982
When Lore Brunner asks me to write something for her, I remember this case and decide to use it as the basis for a dramatic plot. It was to be a 'life of Germany', in monologue form, reflecting the last few decades of German history. Dramatic literature throughout the ages has had recourse to breeches' parts for erotic, but not so far I know, for social purposes.

July/August 1982
In a Provençal holiday villa, surrounded by fields of flowering lavender, at a sufficient distance from the location of the episode, the text of *Jacke Wie Hose* comes into being.

15th December 1982
First night of the play, with Lore Brunner in the role of Max Gericke, at the studio of the Bochum Theatre.

Meanwhile
The play is translated into a number of languages and performed in several countries in Europe. Lore Brunner has performed her interpretation of the role of Max Gericke in theatres throughout the world.

26th January 1987
By sheer coincidence I come across a copy of the newspaper article about the subject of the play. Years later, I am disturbed to find myself looking at the face of the woman whose story had such an impact on me. I am astounded to read that she had succeeded in playing her 'rôle' for twelve years. All along I'd assumed that keeping up the artifice so flawlessly for so long was purely the prerogative of art.
Manfred Karge, Vienna, February 2nd, 1987

(*translated by Tinch Minter and Anthony Vivis*)

Woman disguised as Man for Twelve Years

One day the tax inspectorate discovered that a nightwatchman who had worked diligently at a factory in Mainz for twelve years was a woman. After separating from her husband, she had appropriated his identity papers, disguised herself as a man and applied for a job. She had even acted the rôle of a good family man by getting married in a registry office to a woman with two children. (*Wide World*)

THE CONQUEST OF THE SOUTH POLE
Beyond The Seventh Sea (*Jenseits des Siebenten Meeres*)

People find it easy to use their imaginations for extending the limitations of space, sensing the presence of something beyond the horizon defined by the sea. Even in the far past when people assumed the earth was either a flat disc or one with a slight concavity, they could be led into believing that beyond the girdle formed by the ocean of Homer, lay another place where people could live, with an economy of its own. Like the lokaloka of Indian mythology, they believed in a ring of mountains lying beyond the seventh sea.

Alexander von Humboldt
(*translated by Tinch Minter and Anthony Vivis*)

Man To Man has been performed so far in:
Bochum, Munich, Graz, Vienna, Stuttgart, Brussels, East and West Berlin, Zurich, Paris, Lyons, Erlangen, Lille, Parma, Rome, Geneva, Hanover, Berne, Bonn, Tübingen, Münster, Marburg, Toronto, Cologne, Rio de Janeiro, Darmstadt, Amsterdam, Antwerp, Schwerin, Regensburg, Oslo, Wiesbaden, Saarbrücken, Ljubljana, Edinburgh, Hamburg, Heidelberg, London and Düsseldorf.

The Conquest Of The South Pole has so far been performed in:
Bochum, Brussels, Avignon, Strasbourg, Belfort, Grenoble, Geneva, Cologne, Edinburgh and London.

Manfred Karge

Manfred Karge was born in 1938 in Brandenburg. He worked first at the Berliner Ensemble, then at the Volksbühne, Berlin, both acting and directing with Matthias Langhoff. In addition to his work as a director of classic and contemporary work by writers such as Brecht, Kleist and Brasch, Manfred Karge has written *Man to Man* (1982), *Claire*, a musical, (1985), *The Conquest of the South Pole* (1986) and *Lieber Niembsch* (1988). He will direct the world première of *Lieber Niembsch* (*Dear Niembsch*) in Vienna in 1989.

Note on the Translators

Individually Tinch Minter and Anthony Vivis have written both for and about the theatre. Recent co-translations include Botho Strauss's *The Tourist Guide*, Almeida Theatre (1987) and *The Park*, Sheffield Crucible (1988), and Gerlind Reinshagen's *Sunday's Children*, Derby Playhouse (1988). Their translations range from *Faust* to works by Fassbinder. In 1987 they were awarded an Arts Council Bursary for translations of works by Christine Brückner, Friedrich Dürrenmatt and Felix Mitterer. They have just completed a translation of *Stalin* by Gaston Salvatore, commissioned by the Bush Theatre.